# TINTIN IN THE
# NEW WORLD

# TINTIN IN THE NEW WORLD

## A ROMANCE

## Frederic Tuten

William Morrow and Company, Inc.
*New York*

Chapters of *Tintin in the New World* first appeared in their entire
or altered form in *Fiction* (1975), *Tri-Quarterly* (1975), *Syntaxis*
(1984), *Artforum* (1984), and *De Brakke Hond* (1984).

Frontispiece: *Interior with Painting of Tintin*,
pencil and colored pencils on paper, copyright © 1992
by Roy Lichtenstein. Photographs of frontispiece and jacket
artwork by Robert McKeever.

With grateful acknowledgment to Fanny Remi and the Hergé
Foundation for their permission to use images from *Tintin* on the
dustcover and frontispiece of this edition.

It is the policy of William Morrow and Company, Inc., and its
imprints and affiliates, recognizing the importance of preserving
what has been written, to print the books we publish on acid-free
paper, and we exert our best efforts to that end.

Library of Congress Cataloging-in-Publication Data
Tuten, Frederic.
Tintin in the new world : a romance / Frederic Tuten.—1st ed.
p.   cm.
ISBN 0-688-12314-7
1. Tintin (Fictitious character)—Fiction.   I. Title.
PS3570.U78T56   1993
813'.54—dc20                    92–27276   CIP

Printed in the United States of America

First Edition

1   2   3   4   5   6   7   8   9   10

BOOK DESIGN BY RHEA BRAUNSTEIN

*This novel is dedicated to the memory of my friend George Remi (Hergé) and is offered with love to Dooley Worth, Dorothy Herzka, and Roy Lichtenstein*

*With thanks to the Guggenheim Foundation for its support (1973–1974) in the writing of this book.*

1ST LORD: What time o' day is 't, Apemantus?
APEMANTUS: Time to be honest.

*Timon of Athens* I.i.

—————— Chapter I ——————

"All the winter the north wind roamed on the hills; many trees fell in the park." Marlinspike "seemed barer and more desolate than ever; broken branches littered the roadway, and tall trunks showed their wounds." Beyond the sandstone balustrade, far beyond the tawny, wet dunes and eroded beach, out across the whitecapped sea, a lone fishing boat silhouetted itself against the orangy wintersky, and long sheets of gray clouds heaved on tips of leaden sea-swells. It drizzled. Tintin morosely regarded the blustery scene from his library window.

The tiny ship in the distance made him feel sad, and the rain dispirited him. He had been still for too long, alone in the huge manor with his companions, Captain Haddock and the terrier, Snowy, who was now dreaming in the glow of a fire flaring in the huge stone hearth. Tintin shuffled back to his Morris chair and returned to his book. He read:

Later, I shaved, got dressed and went over to the trailer. The Greek wasn't there but Rose was, in a negligee and red pumps. She looked swell. I came over close. She looked awful. Her shoulder was crisscrossed with welts and her left eye was puffy and blue.

"He was sore, Rex, and he walloped me with a clothesline. It was bad."

"I'll kill him," I said, my stomach sick.

"You better, or he'll get us both."

He was a greasy Greek and he sweated a lot like all those greasers do. He was frying eggs over the grill and he didn't hear me come in, even when the screen door hissed shut. I tucked the .38 away, grabbed an iron skillet off the shelf, and cracked his head hard. He went down on the sawdust. The eggs and hot grease went over him and steamed on his face. He was groaning. I smashed him again. He went out.

I dragged him under the counter. The eggs slid down his face and patted the floor. He wasn't bleeding. I hung the "Return Later" sign over the door and pulled down the shade. I left him there and went back to the trailer.

"Rose, I nailed him."

"Oh, baby," she moaned.

"It's over now. We're free."

She slowly slid out of her negligee. "Oh, yes, baby," she purred. I went over to her. Rose. That's all that mattered.

There it was. Adults! Always the same: all for lust and murder. Thank the stars he knew nothing of that.

I shall always be glad to have stayed stunted at twelve, he thought. Quirk of biological fate—my best luck.

Windows rattled and the fireplace gusted smoke in the chimney downdraft. Snowy slept at Tintin's feet, dreaming of marrow bones heaped in secret caves, dreaming of sudden feints at arrogant crows and hairy villains. Captain Haddock's old ship's barometer sank. For a moment the wind ceased, the air vacuumed; Tintin could scarcely breathe. Then the storm flooded the night.

Tintin put down his novel. Snowy woke, his eyes red-rimmed. "This is no night to be at sea," Captain Haddock mumbled, entering the carpeted room noiselessly.

"No night to be at Marlinspike either," answered Tintin. "We've been home too long with too little to do. I'm tired of reading, tired of long strolls, tired of tranquil evenings before the fire. How can you bear it? Not one adventure, not one exploit in ages. I'm too young to stay still for so long. You've got your whiskey to comfort you, Captain, and you've got your old man's memories to keep you agog through the dead months."

"Old age? Auguring asteroids! I'm not yet fifty. Tintin, my lad, if you'd learn to drink scotch and love women, you, too, would have cheering memories in old age!"

"I have no feeling for either."

"How do you know till you've experienced them?"

*Yes,* Snowy thought, *why doesn't he try? Maybe he'll grow up a bit and stay home more.*

"Captain, enough. Let's find something practical to do."

"To do? You've *everything* to do here at Marlinspike. Last month you bought two Arabian steeds and rode them an inch to foamy death, now you hardly give 'em a glance when you pass the stables. They'll soon melt into glue. Then there's the observatory you had erected with a telescope strong enough to see the hairs in God's long nose. 'I've exhausted the heavens,' you said after seven hours of ripping through the skies."

"I'm restless by nature," Tintin said, in a sad whisper.

"Blustering bananas! My dear Tintin, you are perfectly *unsettled*! My heart breaks to see you in such a funk."

"What to do? There's an urge in me to be on the move, to set this wrong world right. Do you realize it's a year since we last adventured?"

"What about your art collecting? Have you given that up, too? All those unopened crates of paintings you've left unexamined: that Matisse you spent ages to acquire—that one with all those naked dancing people—still in its shipping case. Tintin, this house is littered with the goods of your discontent."

*One juicy marrow bone keeps me glad for days,* thought Snowy, turning on his back to let his pink belly bask in the fire's hot glow. *Humans are peculiar, need so much.*

"Let's take a holiday, Captain, a short trip to the High Atlas or maybe Wyoming."

"My boy, let's steer truer to course. 'Tis no journey you now need. I fear there's something incomplete in you."

"We've been through that, Captain. I'm content in every way, and the other thing, well, I feel nothing for it, so don't miss or want it."

"By Orion's teeth! I've been boy and man at sea, kept a narrow 'n' solitary bunk and wished for none else, yet at times, when the sky washed golden and the sea flattened itself level into a plate of blue, when an island loomed like a ripe persimmon on the horizon, I sometimes wished my briny soul softened by woman's touch. A girl from home country, I mean, none of your port trollops. Yes. A true country girl! Then she would come and say me, 'Oh! Captain, my dear, do come to table.' And there would be waiting my steaming lamb pie and me weatherglass of malt, neat, filled to brim's edge. And this lovely plump, rosy woman, my own wifey, does bend to kiss me on my cheek as I make to tie my napkin 'bout my neck.

"And perhaps, too, there'd be some little Haddocks swimming around me ankles, little ones all glowing and proud of their big papa. . . . 'And what's the wisest fish in the sea, me children?' I'd ask, with a grave, schoolmasterish frown on my face. 'Old Haddock! Old Haddock!' they'd answer in glee.

"I miss this dear wifey I shall never know. My life charts are fixed now—too late to alter course—but I sometimes think I should have planned for warm, fertile shelter at journey's end. Yet there's time ahead left for you to share such homey joys as those I've missed."

"Captain," Tintin said impatiently, "I offer you my final words on this matter. I've read about the subject you raise, 'bout how men hurl themselves off cliffs or blow out their brains or kill other men over the love of a girl. *So,* what is it I have missed? Sorrow? Do you remember that season we went to every opera at La Scala and Bayreuth. Those operas where girl and boy meet, fall in love; then, when one leaves the other, the deserted one moans, cries to heaven and to hell or joins a band of outlaws."

*Seldom hear Tintin talk so much. I like him better when he's chasing villains or getting out of a scrape.*

"Wait! I forgot," Tintin continued. "Then there's always the case of two who are in love, but one dies, leaving the other in terrible despair, always ready to sob in the street or while strolling alone in a zoo. If death does not divide lovers, it's something else, a war or TB. Sorrow is what love teaches, so what's to gain in this swamp of weepy roses?"

"Where's my bottle?"

"There on the floor, by the Ming vase, where you left it two hours ago."

"And now that you have clarified your sentiments and left me no room to finish my theme," Captain Haddock said sententiously, pouring whiskey into a cup, "I may as well tell you, one of *those* letters came by messenger this afternoon while you were out scouting about the estate."

"The same cream-white envelope?"

"As ever. Here," said Captain Haddock, removing the letter from the side pocket of his gold-buttoned blue blazer.

Tintin recognized the stationery and the address at the right-hand corner: "Avenue du Vert Chasseur, Bruxelles." In whatever remote part of the world Tintin found himself, the writer had known where to reach him to signal him to an adventure. Tintin perceived immediately that this missive was different from all the others, which, in their tone and brevity, seemed almost brusque commands. It began:

> *Mon cher* Tintin, for some time our destinies have linked, yours and mine. I have directed your pursuits, leaving you, however, in the time not taken by some mission at hand, to plot your own stars. I do not know how kind those stars have been to you or how well or wisely you have followed them; all that is beyond my power and past my design. But in those matters in which I have influence, I have seen to it that you've been the instrument of good service to this planet. Always you have been sincere and intrepid. Were you the child of my own blood and not the personage of my dreams, I could wish for no better. But once we are born and once set on path, there's more splendid uncertainty for each of us, not least among us you. Thus, I'm told, even God and his knowing stars create and direct and foreknow the end, yet the route itself and the journey's reach no one but the destined traveler may choose, though the whole map be drawn and charted to our lastmost step.
>
> I myself know little of the prospect before you, except that it shall be of consequence to you. Follow now your

destined but alterable track, which begins at Machu Picchu, Peru. Go there now.

"I see by your expression we're at it again," Captain Haddock said glumly.

"Not a moment too soon," Tintin exultantly replied.

Snowy yawned. An ancient oak crashed in the park.

# Chapter II

[Prow side, Tintin alone. Eight bells. Wind, N by NW, (Apollo's wind). Snowy parades the deck, his snout aloft, sniffing the aroma of brine and dolphins.]

"Come, come, Snowy, here by me. Look up, my boy, see Orion and his dog, Sirius, and there—no, no, there!—the Dipper so large and so low as to seem ready to ladle the ocean. What a mighty sky tonight."

*The world's dream plays in the sky, but he can't quite see it, though with his child's eyes and child's heart he comes closer to perceiving it than any other human I know. I love him and will keep beside him.*

"Yes, Snowy, it makes one think about things, doesn't it?—about how this watery world came to be made and what is the sense of it, to be going on always this way, from one episode of right doing to another, to what final end, I ask . . . though I've never asked this before. Yes, to what end? I ask. Snowy, look there. A phosphorescent question mark gleams dully in our ship's roiling wake. Is it a glowing sign of reply or is this milky mark a picture echo of my thoughts projected on high?"

*The night's sea and sky offer him a terrific theme, and soon, I fear, like those of his human kin, even he will burst rhapsodic and strain to lofty spheres. Oh, Tintin, brother animal whom I love, stay the animal that you are, and leave aside these extravagant sensations and thoughts. Don't trouble yourself with dreamy troubles, let humans be humans and dogs dogs. There's no matter beyond that, I say.*

—————— Chapter III ——————

[Some weeks later. The port of Callao, Peru.]

Pilings, moorings, fastening of stout lines to lead cleats, the chainy letting-down of anchors, the rush of ship's crew and harbor porters, the uneasy tremble of body as Tintin first steps again on land.

The valise-piled quay, the silver-gray Rolls and capped chauffeur, the settling of luggage in trunk, the silent ride through the luxurious quarters of town. Snowy, his eyes wide, his ears pricked, his snout sniffing the open window space; Haddock listless, his beard flounced; Tintin alert, his hearing the phrase, "It's breaking, it's the cliff for me, too, then"—the voice his own. They arrive.

The Grand Hotel of Lima. Politeness at the front desk. Señor Tintin has been expected. Manager, in morning coat, tails, and pinstripe, pants' cuffs drooping to his heels, assistants in blue suits, uniformed porters (lots drawn weeks earlier for the privilege of carrying the young detective's suitcases), the entire staff seen and unseen, in halls and kitchens, out in the gardens and by the pool, waiting for him.

But no word for him at the desk, no letter or note of instructions. Nothing as well the following morning, when Tintin leaves for Cuzco, the middle of his journey.

## Chapter IV

[A day later. Cuzco, Peru: Stop-off point en route to Tintin's appointed destination, the Inca ruins and little hotel of Machu Picchu.

Street market. 8:30 A.M. Snowy investigates the meat stalls, sniffs about the legs of tethered burros, and finally takes a position beside a blind Indian beggar squatting beneath a makeshift canopy.]

*There's dogs and dogs. Not only size, I mean. But ways of life, mastered or masterless, pampered or kicked about. This is no country for dogs here. Always can tell 'bout a place by the way my fellow dogs are doing. Too many cripples and lean ones here. Too much scrounging about for a lick of bone, too much mange and rheumy snouts, too many sunken eyes and tails between the legs—means trouble, kids stoning 'em and cars ready to run 'em over in the streets for sport. Better hug close to Tintin and the old drunk, else I'll end up in a stewpot. Creatures my size ain't got much chance.*

*Oh! Look, she, there, sleek, her petite nose a little stuck up in the air but her eyes big and sad, got a mean master perhaps, or maybe she's got worms. Must get closer and sniff her out, don't want to seem too forward, though, especially here where the etiquette is unfamiliar to me. Must be careful here. Not like walking with Tintin or the captain and casually sidling up to a fine miss for a good whiff. Must be careful here.*

—————— Chapter V ——————

[Two days later. The hotel of Machu Picchu, huddled among its ancient stone ruins, six thousand feet above sea level. Oxygen level thin. Guest capacity, twenty. Staff present, six. Telephone none. 7:30 A.M.]

When he woke, Tintin did not know where he was. His head and chest ached, and little white specks skidded before his eyes. He looked about the sunlit room for a familiar sign and found none. Thinking he was still in his hotel room in Cuzco and still dizzy from the altitude, he peered over the edge of the bed for the familiar green tube of oxygen, but he discovered only his maroon slippers at the blue carpet's edge. For some moments he felt so disoriented that he wondered whether or not he was a child again, that same child who frequently woke in the chilled dark of early morning, frightened that his mother had abandoned him or had died and that he was alone forever in the dark house of this large lonely world. At the very instant when he felt most abject, when he began to fall into the familiar spin of this particular and recurrent anguish, Captain Haddock entered the room with Snowy at his cuffs.

"Why, Captain, I'm so glad to see you, and you, too, dear Snowy!" Tintin exclaimed. "I was so puzzled, and now here you are, thank heavens, to solve it all. We're here, aren't we, Captain?"

"Here, and never to fall off the planks of this globe, me lad. You're looking bilish, as if you'd downed a cask of peppery brine."

"I'll soon be as bright as a razor. Just let me see your faces, dear friends and let me hear your morning bark, good Snowy, why, yes, then I'll shine like the new day sun itself."

*It's his fit,* thought Snowy, letting out a long howl of greeting, *the misery-mama fit that comes over all of them, young and old, 'n' it's this fit that proves them so crazy no matter how sensible they seem, for when we folks leave the den, it's over and done and there's no remembering or hankering after that old time, but these human creatures moan all their lives over for that lost den and those delicious wet teats, wanting ever and again mommy's little muzzle and her little nudges and nips. And they dare, these humans, talk of us always clinging and hungry for love, for a kick, even, so long as it's our loving master's foot that finds our backsides. Well, I do pity him. I can't show him enough affection when it comes to this type of fit.*

"What you need's a good breakfast, me boy, and that'll start this day smooth again," said Haddock.

"You choose for me, please," Tintin answered dreamily, "and order for me some pure water from some high mountain stream, some secret rivulet whose source is known only to the just and the sane. There! From that very bubbling cleft I now see beside the jaguar's cave, some seven miles from this place."

"Just so," Haddock assented, glancing warily at his companion, "and perhaps some fruit juice and toast while we are at it. And perhaps a breath or two of tanked oxygen after breakfast. Why, I'll even join you in a few deep breaths of that heady stuff. The air's too fine for my thick head."

"No need for oxygen, Captain, not for me, at least—I'm feeling quite myself again. I wish to explore these hills and ruins straight after breakfast and learn the territory of our present campaign. Remain here if you feel tired."

Bewildered by Tintin's sudden shifts of mood and thought, Captain Haddock kept his counsel, and without another word they sped to the dining room, where they took the last vacant table in the small room. Their entrance created no stir, the other breakfasters seeming to remain attentive to their morning dishes and to one another, although a woman of olive skin and long, silver-streaked black hair did incline her head slightly toward Tintin as he brushed by her table.

A voice from that woman's table rose above the common din.

"*Sapristi!* I declare all truces broken with this man."

"Break, break, break all you please," came another cry, "for you are a people who respect no pacts or treaties, and therefore all agreements made with your kind are a priori null and void."

"As I thought, you had no intention of respecting our agreement from the start, you of the treacherous and bellicose race."

"Nonsense," bellowed a voice more commanding than the others, "we'll have no quarrels today."

Turning rapidly to locate the source of the disturbance, Tintin caught the eyes of a large, bearded man just as the man's thick fist slammed on the table. Silverware and plates jumped, coffee erupted from the trembling cups. In the silence that followed—for all the breakfasters in the room had immediately turned still—the olive-skinned woman's voice filled the room. "Excuse us for the little tumult, fellow guests, my rowdy friends here ask your pardon, I'm sure."

In response, a young caballero, his pomaded black hair gleaming, rose from a distant table and, as if representing all present, ventured a speech in English. "Madame, your beauty would make us all rowdy, your charm and loveliness make us obedient to all your wishes, to pardon Satan should you ask."

He suddenly sat himself down, apparently surprised by his own boldness, for his words seemed to come not so much from practiced flattery as from some urgent need, more powerful than his own reserve, to make his existence known to the woman.

Sounds of approval, some guttural, some high-pitched, some falsetto, some bass, played through the room; some thumped their tables with spoons and forks to signal their approval of the young man's gallantry, but in one corner, a coarse remark stained the convivial air.

Tintin saw the caballero redden, rise, and rush to the table of the offending wit, a portly man who had returned to his grapefruit unaware of the youth standing over him.

Whatever the youth hissed to the older man was inaudible to Tintin, but the words instantly galvanized the jokester, who rose and bowed apologetically in the direction of the table that had originated the commotion.

Clearly mollified, though flustered, the avenging cavalier returned to his seat and busied himself, his eyes downcast, with awkward and exaggerated precision, to the affair of pouring his coffee and buttering his toast.

"A squall in a nun's thimble," mumbled Haddock, "but now me plate is glacial, and I think I'll take myself to more warming refreshments."

Tintin did not reply but distractedly went about wringing his napkin.

"Yes, back to me bottle," Haddock persisted.

But this, too, did not provoke a response, and some further moments passed before Tintin spoke.

"Those people seem very interesting, don't you think?" whispered Tintin earnestly.

"How so, my lad? Many such windy passengers have freighted my mess since I captained at sea. It's best to ignore 'em and leave 'em to their fussing, or they'll soon climb up your jammers and nest in your pockets."

"Yes, I suppose. You know the traveling world, and you know its combinations, yet there are voices . . . sounds that enter one's lonely cells as do no others, their very timbre, pitch, tenor, and texture so unique as to unlock one's bolted soul, the 'open sesame' of sounds lifting the stony lid of one's guarded, secret cave. *Your* voice, for example, Captain, charged with brine and cold seas, with the wet dust of foggy nights and cold watch, comforts me. These past minutes I've heard an unusual voice, the claiming voice of that enchanting woman. . . . "

"It tells you what, me boy?

" 'That once we rose up slowly as if we did not belong to the outside world any longer—like swimmers in a shadowy dream who do not need to breathe.' "

"Your words and thoughts lie beyond my soundings, grow more unfathomable each passing day," said Haddock, shaken. "Let's leave this place. Oh, let's go away before bad things happen."

"Attention, Captain!" Tintin answered playfully. "Let no man jump his watch, lest it hurtle him through time's wide pipes."

"Would you stroll with me then, lad, and guide me through these parts and ruins and take Snowy by our side, for he always quickens you to yourself, more than I, at times?"

"Oh, yes, Captain. Let's find that dog and be on our way."

# Chapter VI

[Midday. Tintin, Captain Haddock, and Snowy pause after strolling among the ruins of the ancient Inca city.]

"I have no love for these fat stones," said Haddock, seating himself at the base of an Inca wall, "as indeed, I care not for your general ruins, your tall Greek pillars and profound Roman baths, your squat medieval towers, your bulky old hulks of olden times, they throw me into a blistering funk, these do."

"Well, I must say, Captain, astonishing as these Inca walls are and marvel-filled as this part of the globe is, I do feel time's awasting, and I'm no closer to knowing what I was sent here for than when we left Marlinspike. But as for the ruins themselves, they serve to instruct and to edify; at least that is what I've read. Our guidebook teaches me what these stones mean and gives me news of what was and what has happened here."

"It fills my becalmed sails to hear you speak of history; read to me, then."

Tintin opened his book, a guide to South America, and flipped through its pages, thinking to read relevant passages to his companion, but Snowy barked his warning bark as a man approached. Tintin looked up to see a lean man in military uniform standing over him.

"Good afternoon, Señor Tintin. I am Lieutenant Nelson dos Amantes, *a sus órdenes*. Excuse this interruption of your privacy, but I have been elected to ask you to join a few of us for lunch."

# Chapter VII

Tintin's heart fluttered. There they were, the rowdy group of the breakfast table, now reassembled for the midday meal. All rose, save the woman, to greet the arrivals. The large, bearded man bowed; the short man clicked his heels; the third, lean and tall, merely extended his hand to no one in particular. Herr Peeperkorn, Herr Naptha, and Signor Settembrini they were, in that order. The woman languidly disposed at the table (her eyes downcast, her arms elongated on the white cloth) was Madame Chauchat, or so Tintin understood from Herr Peeperkorn's bellowed introduction.

Whatever her name, it was she. She of the olive skin, the she to whom the brave caballero had—in the face of the world—delivered his compliments. She, whose voice purred of autumn leaves rasping across a grate, spoke.

"It is generous of you and your companion to join us today. You are, after all, famous the world over for your reserve."

"Shyness, madame," Tintin heard himself say, his voice far away from him.

"Nonsense, young sir," Peeperkorn said, "there is no cause for shyness. Expanse, the fluid and natural flow of conver-

sation, I enjoin you, are our custom here. Sit, stride a chair.
Eat."

They were, excepting the lieutenant, travelers whose paths
had crossed and crossed again over the years. Madame
Clavdia Chauchat, Peeperkorn explained, was his traveling
companion, his indulgent comrade in life's adventures ever
since they had met—where? On the Russian steppes, the coffee plantations of Java?—and had passed a tonic winter together in the Alps, where they had the pleasure of
encountering Signor Settembrini and Herr Naptha, fellow
sojourners on the mountain heights. Amusing and entertaining and very instructive fellows they were, too, each given
to high thinking and speculation, the life of the mind, you
know.

Signor Settembrini, if he, Peeperkorn, be allowed to speak
for him, edits the renowned, but of limited circulation, *Re-
view of Human Suffering,* dedicated to investigating the causes
of and solutions to the discontent and misery of the species;
humanism and science, progress and democracy are the journal's bywords, the betterment of the human condition its aim.

"You simplify too much," Settembrini interjected. "Our
new friends here should have the opportunity to hear my
case and judge for themselves the range and merits of my
beliefs, which have undergone changes over the years."

"Nothing of your simpleminded notions matter, however
much you reform and revise them," Naptha said acidly.

And this, then, was Herr Naptha. How to describe him?
Peeperkorn, for the sake of his new friends, would try. Herr
Naptha has been expounding for years the virtues of a society
whose economic base is Communist and whose spiritual and
governmental principles are Roman Catholic—Herr Naptha
himself being a Jesuit on extended leave from his order.

"Mention, too, that your Settembrini is a Freemason, and of some high degree, I suspect," Naptha said. "In any case, much has changed for me as well, since the days we spoke. I've come to different thoughts and have long since been independent of any orders, religious or otherwise."

"Our good lieutenant here must speak for himself," Herr Peeperkorn said, continuing his introductions, "for I know very little except that he is intelligent, a military man stationed to protect these regions and this ancient site, a man bent on reform, and a man of his people, if I understand him correctly."

"You understand very well, sir," the lieutenant answered, "though I should clarify that my people are the native and the original inhabitants of these mountains and of this land you Europeans call Peru."

"Are you, too, a reformer?" Tintin asked the woman, from whom he could not take his eyes.

"Yes, she, too." Peeperkorn laughed. "She reforms my wallet by reducing it, though I wish she could do for my person what she does to my purse, transforming fat to lean."

Madame Chauchat blanched and made to rise from the table.

"No, no," Peeperkorn protested, "do not leave. Clavdia, I ask your pardon before all here. A stupid remark without a jot of substance or truth made for the sake of the joke on myself. I beg the pardon of all for my vulgar lapse."

"I myself am not offended," Settembrini said.

"Nor I," Naptha said, "though it is strange to find myself agreeing with the signor here."

"Is it not for the lady to accept the apology?" Lieutenant dos Amantes asked.

"But of course, it is!" exclaimed Tintin, slapping his forehead. "What a ninny I am not to have thought of that."

"No harm, gentlemen," Clavdia said graciously. "But still I shall leave."

"I ask that you remain among us here," Tintin said. "Your withdrawal would devastate the day."

Captain Haddock fidgeted and let out a deep sigh. Snowy, who was busy sniffing the aromas of pants legs and shoes under the table, stopped for a moment and pricked his ears. *He likes the lady. I'll give her a whiff and smell her out for him. Double caution's needed up here where the air's so nothing.*

"Ah! How can you refuse your cavalier," Peeperkorn said, "for his sake if not for mine?"

"I shall stay then," Clavdia said, addressing Tintin, "if only to hear your thoughts at our little symposium."

"Resolved! How wonderful that we are composed at table again! Joy! Total!" Peeperkorn exclaimed. "A restful and solid finale to all struggles is the table, a life ending in bounty and grace. Yes. Many would have it otherwise, burning, you know, flashing cometlike through the final years, drink perhaps, or the needle or the deep draw of the opium pipe, or all three—though I exaggerate, surely not all, too many spices in that broth to distinguish any flavor. Now, as we were saying, how I begin my day.

"In the morning, a thick blue jug of steaming cocoa, thick slabs of buttered and marmaladed toast on a blue-rimmed stone plate, all taken while propping oneself against the bed's mountainous pillows. Sunlight, champagne pale through the window, warming the face and arms and breast, for one's nether parts are yet under the quilt; then the papers, read page by tasty page. Perhaps, too, a cut of seasoned ham, and eggs, lightly peppered atop the gelatinous frame of the yellow jell. Coffee, a mixture of—"

"As I began to say at breakfast," Naptha interjected, "one

mustn't forget that above all, Marx was a polemicist. His economic theories are hardly relevant today, as regards real life, I mean. But enough, this is all common knowledge, and besides, none of this interests me greatly any longer."

"You are too coy, my dear friend," Settembrini said caustically. "But for the sake of Tintin and Captain Haddock, our new friends, I shall play your game and ask, Pray, what does interest you?"

"As always, man's soul. Which is the same nearly everywhere. The seeming inequity of state or private capitalism no longer disturbs me, for exploitation and privilege have been and ever shall be the condition of any society."

"You have changed your canzone over these years, Mr. Naptha! How long ago was it you were dreamily extolling the virtues of and the necessity for what shall we call it?—a spiritual, a transcendental communism? Yes, once you preached religion and common ownership of property, a real *minestrone* of ideas, indeed; the city of God run under scientific principles."

"I do admit to a certain amount of former ideological immaturity," Naptha answered, "but one must change along with the conditions of life, though *you* do not seem to, spouting, as you do, the same old dishwater of universal peace and progress through the advancement of learning and reason. And you, who so dearly wish the world's good, seem not to manage very well his own welfare. I notice your trousers are still thin at the seat and frayed at the cuffs."

By coincidence, Snowy had just arrived, at that instant, at Settembrini's pants cuffs and was inhaling the rich aroma of lint and stale bread crumbs. Settembrini looked down in fear.

"He will have my ankle, this dog. Can't we put him out, Signor Tintin?"

"Have no fear, this is a good hound; he smells the rodent in its lair," Naptha said.

"Come stay beside me, Monsieur Snowy," Clavdia said. "Or take my lap for your seat if it please you."

Snowy glanced toward Tintin for advice and, finding a nod of assent, went off to the woman, who was setting down some sugar cubes for him beside her chair.

*The world's richer for her. I'll like her till I don't.*

"We were not discussing my sartorial situation, sir," Settembrini answered. "When you are cornered in your vulnerable intellectual hole, you resort to petty argument *ad hominem,* but our friends here, I'm sure, discern your shabby little ploy."

"No offense intended. Only to say that the world changes but you remain the same, while I at least, attempt to tailor myself with contemporary cloth. Shortly ago you accused me of a former dreaminess regarding the world, and I agreed. Today I know it is better to accept than to prescribe the conditions of reality. Who am I to beat the sea with chains?"

"Shameless man!" Settembrini exclaimed. "Insane as it may have been, at least your former dream had the virtue of reform, but now you tell us that you take the world for what it is, that you accept wickedness and wrongdoing and unreason."

"Do you mean, Señor Naptha, that you countenance the exploitation of the poor and of the workers who create the world's wealth?" asked Lieutenant dos Amantes.

"Lieutenant, I answer you thus: 'There are classes of men in the world who bear the same relation to society at large that the wheels do to a coach and are just as indispensable. You may legislate the number of passengers, so that the coach does not groan under their weight, or you may increase the number of wheels, so that both the conveyance and the riders may progress more easily, but in whatever combination, there must always be a coach and its wheels, else there is no movement.' And since I prefer to ride rather than to be ridden on, I take appropriate measures. You, my dear lieutenant, ask only that the wheels exchange places with the passengers."

"*Dove c'è equagliànza non c'è lucro,*" commented Settembrini. "Which I translate, 'Where there is equality there is no profit.' Thus—"

"Thus, nothing," Naptha blurted. "For I answer you: *Nil posse creari de nihilo,* 'from nothing, nothing is created.' "

"Excuse me, gentlemen, I am losing your drift," Tintin said.

"It's no matter," Clavdia interjected. "When men gather, except when a woman they wish to charm is present, they always prattle about money."

"I mean," continued Tintin, letting pass Clavdia's comment, "this business of the coach and its wheels doesn't apply today because we've got airplanes."

"At last a sensible, modern voice," Clavdia exclaimed, bestowing a smile on the young man.

"You misrepresent me, Señor Naptha. Awhile ago you suggested I wish only to transform the oppressors into slaves and the slaves into masters. This is not true, as you yourself probably know."

"And what, then, *would* you desire, Lieutenant?" Settembrini inquired, turning attentively to the young officer.

"Things for us here are elemental. We require the elimination of the latifundia and the ownership of huge estates by absentee landlords; we must return to the communal system of our ancestors. The Indians must have their ancient lands and language returned to them; they must be self-governing, autonomous, tribal, yet ultimately connected to the whole of our culture."

"What you would like then is a form of pre-Columbian, Inca civilization mixed with the blessings of modern technology and science," Settembrini interjected condescendingly.

"Perhaps that," the lieutenant replied, averting his eyes from the speaker.

"In short, you propose fascism."

"That is a specialty reserved for Italians," the lieutenant answered curtly.

"Fascism, sir, is a generic term, applicable to all states bent on nationalism and state socialism, on a retrograde and mystical love of the folk blended with elitism and economic and political tyranny."

The lieutenant drew his chair back abruptly and remained silent for a moment, as did the others at the table. Suddenly the officer erupted: "Names of things do not apply. *Eso no significa nada, usted habla de cosas que no significan nada hoy. Estamos todavía en la garra del pasado, bajo su tiranía. Necesitamos una vida nueva, sin extranjeros, ni las ideas del mundo viejo. Todo será nuevo aquí, en el porvenir todo será nuevo.*"

"Yes, of course," Peeperkorn said, "in the future all shall be new, no sadness, none. Pretty children and pretty mothers, land fertile, sunshine, ever-golden days. No ugliness, none. Neither illness nor aging, not a graying hair in the lot, but all as youths and maidens—well built, you understand, magnificent bodies all. There shall I go, where good manners and grace count for something. Let's go."

*I would like that, a place where dogs can be dogs once and for all. Dog Land: bones strewn along mossy paths, hills of silken leaves to tumble in, packs of sleek-haired bitches in furnace heat, griffons, and giant Irish wolfhounds even, who won't turn their noses up at a runt like me. Yes, my kind of place.*

"Rather ride than be ridden on!" shouted Settembrini, his mind suddenly returned to Naptha's coach metaphor. "In fact, you actually benefit from this vehicle of capitalism. Everyone knows of your wealth, however modestly you seem to apply it to your person. Your economic and spiritual determinism is only a grandiose rationale for comfort."

"Well, why not? Only the wastrel leaves fertile fields untilled," Naptha answered. "Yes, through husbandry, patience, and care I have cultivated my well-being, a modest but steady harvest of incomes, reaped from various fertile investments: real estate, of course . . . mutual funds, bonds and securities, and recently some investments with various Brazilian companies—the military keeps things stable there, you know. And there are other minor but firm commitments such as a rent-yielding apartment on the Place des Vogges, Paris."

"Quite adequate, quite a nifty little purse, silk-lined, I may add. Sufficient. Intellectuals require no more; thoroughly rounded, yet with a hint of the austere, the Spartan, the nonaggressive yet bountiful portfolio. You show good taste, Herr Naptha, nothing presumptuous, none of your shaky little deals, none. I, Peeperkorn, approve."

"Disgusting," Settembrini screeched, "money kills thought."

"I don't know too much about the way things are handled for me," Tintin explained, "a man in New York takes care of it, but some of the gold bullion Haddock and I discovered at Marlinspike several years ago is deposited in a Swiss bank. Isn't that so, Captain?"

"Thundering clams! What? The tide's in, you say? Bring her to port and reef the halyards."

"I think the captain is the wisest man here," Clavdia remarked.

The comment was generally ignored, except by Tintin, who beamed at Clavdia's approval of his comrade. Before Tintin could thank her, Settembrini spoke again.

"You have no faith in man, Herr Naptha, or in man's works. And as you have just admitted, your personal interests shape your vision of humanity as a whole."

"As whose does not?" answered Naptha. "Is poverty truth's companion? I go further. History is the story of victims and victors. The question is, Which do you choose to be?"

"Neither. Simply a just man. A man of faith and progress. Even you will admit history has its bright pages among the dark."

"Yes," Naptha answered, "the days when each man knew his place."

"Progress, sir, is the record of men who did not know their place."

"You have just recited the story of Cain and Abel," Naptha said triumphantly.

"All this means nothing to me," the lieutenant interjected. "You both explicate outmoded texts. We are a new world here and require new handbooks and histories, written by ourselves."

"Yes," Peeperkorn said. "Yesterday has no meaning, and certainly not someone else's. Take the course as it comes. One's history begins anew each new day."

"Rarely have I seen you so huffed, dear Peeperkorn, one would almost think you have grown serious here in these rare mountains."

"My Clavdia, I take your observation as a just admonishment; one should not dwell on these matters or on any elevated chats for too long, except for the kind one would have enjoyed at the court of Urbino, when ladies and courtiers made their evening conversation all sympathy and wit."

"But they spoke chiefly of love! No offense, sir, but we were on more significant issues," Naptha interjected, looking at the others for support.

"Still, decorum, comportment, the economy of behavior, grace," Peeperkorn said.

"Are mortified issues!" Settembrini exploded. "With all deference, you are referring to the most decadent of times; others tilled the fields by day, so that these splendid gentle-people could converse at night. Madame Clavdia is wrong: You are never serious, Herr Peeperkorn."

Conversation halted momentarily, while the waiter brought more coffee and the busboy cleared away the re-maining dishes and little pots of butter.

"Those words of yours, Señor Peeperkorn, 'decorum,' 'grace,' " said Lieutenant dos Amantes, "move me to mem-ories of a comrade of my youth, the son of a rich Chinese family. He was born here and shared with us our dreams, though the color of his skin and his class origins made him seem alien to us. I loved him in the way young people are mad for those they wish to resemble. His was a grace and intelligence without mannerism; his calm presence alone shamed loudmouths and revolutionary braggarts among us. He went to the university to please his parents, to respect them, and he studied tropical medicine, but his education was wide, and he read English and French. I think he wrote po-etry. Whatever he did, the revolution was always his calling, his mission.

"For organizing workers in a paper mill, he was arrested and tortured. Fortunately his family was able to obtain his release by bribing officials. He returned to us much changed, very thin and very wasted, but he had no care for how he looked because he was seized by a new idea. 'While I was in

my prison cell,' he said to me, 'I often had a strange vision—
even when I was being beaten, I had this vision. I saw a wide
river walled on either bank by huge, leafy trees. The river
sent voices to me, telling me to wait by this wide river until
I no longer need wait.'

"That was all he ever told me of his prison experience, and
that was the last time I ever spoke to him. When last heard
from, he was in Brazil, on the bank of an Amazon settlement,
working in a laundry.

"*Bueno,* forgive my nostalgia," Lieutenant dos Amantes
said, returning to Peeperkorn's earlier remarks on the need
to reject the past as influence on the present. "You urge us
to live without your history at our backs, but first you
drenched us in Christ's blood, teaching the Indian to be meek,
to suffer his disgusting life with eyes rolled heavenward, now
you extol him to take up the gun in order to create a radical
paradise on earth. You Europeans have bestowed on us all
your failed dreams, hoping they would sprout and flourish
on this new, fertile continent."

"In truth, Lieutenant," said Settembrini, "you are in error.
Look to your New World brothers of the North. Our little
infections, as you term them, are mild colds compared with
those the Yankees have shipped you—real poxes and plagues.
One bottle of Coca-Cola contains more spiritual microbes
than all the boatloads of Marx and Engels."

"Incidentally, do you know," playfully inquired the officer, "that we have our own carbonated beverage, Inca Cola?"

All laughed or smiled indulgently, except Captain Haddock, who napped in his chair, dreaming of crystal skies and
steady winds, his schooner, with spinnaker ballooning prow-
ward, quaffing the sea.

"Why not learn from us, Lieutenant?" Settembrini asked.
"Surely our history cannot count for nothing. All men at all

times have been prone to error, but we have had our noble, inspired moments worthy of emulation by a people intent on progress and justice and harmony."

"You are a worthy man, Señor Settembrini. Yes, an honest man. I do not dismiss your history; indeed, I have read something of it. But nothing, no, little of what you have achieved is of value to us. We are a different people, a different race, a different destiny. Old World analogies do not apply."

"I agree"—Naptha nodded—"but I would go further. Nationalize, socialize; preserve and create your cultural boundaries, build new highways, tame and drain the Amazon, feed the poor, educate them, and give them newspapers. And so? Will you have altered men's souls? Will you have made them less aggressive, less murderous? No, you will only have made more men discontented, each wanting more than his neighbor, and there is no end to wanting."

"When our people want to live, you call us bad," the lieutenant answered, "but when your people grow rich in the manner we wish to pursue, you call it good. What you allow us is our misery, because misery is so cheap that even the poor can afford it."

"Don't listen to him, Lieutenant. Don't trouble yourself, fortunately his mischief is harmless," Settembrini said. "As you know, I have apprehensions about the chauvinism of your programs, but I do not doubt you will find your way, as have others in the past."

"The past, our past, may indeed point the course of our future, Señor Settembrini. There is a story, dating to the preconquest, a part of which I'm sure you know. Long before the Spanish arrived, the Indians believed that one day a man with golden hair, a man half-animal, would appear from the West, sent by Viracocha, the Creator. Pizarro was taken to be that demigod of their legends, and even the great Inca

Atahualpa believed, when he heard reports of the existence of white men on the coast of what we now call Panama, that the prophecy had come true.

"But this is only a fragment of the story. According to another, a heretical account, the arrival of this golden god would bring disorder, destruction, and subjugation, but his reign was predetermined to last only several centuries. During this period the Indians must endure their fate, keeping as much as they can of their language and their culture. For one day, another, more powerful god will appear, to unite them and all their kind from Tierra del Fuego to the northernmost limits of their culture. And this divinity will restore to them their rightful lands and their ancient arts, and afterward he will vanish like rain in the desert. One variation of the story claims that this divinity will unite all the races—that is, all those who now live in the Americas—and that a new kind of man shall emerge.

"Some say this new god is a man; some, a woman; some androgynous. Some believe he will be very young or very old, or both at once. The signs of the coming are known to a few, only by Indians who have had the secret transmitted to them from a line of descent extending back before the great empires of the Aztecs, Mayans, and Incas, before the civilizations of the Toltec, Olmeca, the Chimu, from the time after the great fire and flood, from the time we were first baked from God's clay."

"That is a charming tale," Settembrini said, "one perfectly inspirational in keeping the masses in servitude. Its message: Practice stoicism until the messiah delivers you out of bondage. And notice the Pan-Americanism of it, race and nationalism over again and, of course, the mythic leader. Frankly, it makes me ill."

"Race is the common denominator of all our allegiances

after the family, and the nation after that," Naptha retorted, sneering.

"My friends, not again, please," Peeperkorn pleaded. "We have such charming, lucid company with us this afternoon. Lieutenant, you are to be thanked for entertaining us with such an unusual tale, a story enriching all who have listened. But now to some champagne and cold beef."

"I thank you, too, Lieutenant dos Amantes," said Tintin shyly. "Since I've arrived in your part of the world, my mind seems to be drifting willy-nilly, and I've dreamed of a stable bed on which to fix my wayward thoughts. So fascinating is the subject on which you speak that I expect to give it some study and, thus, perhaps ground myself in thoughts historical and cultural pertaining to this new world."

Lieutenant dos Amantes nodded gravely at the conclusion of Tintin's appreciative words.

"One day I would welcome hearing more of these mystifications," Settembrini intruded, "seeing, after all, that we are respectful guests in your enchanted country. Fables apart, however, as I began to say earlier, there are historical models in our European culture for the kind of society one should wish to realize in the future."

From there Settembrini declaimed on the nature of republics and on the origin and history of the loftiest, Venice, the diadem of the Adriatic, the saving beacon in a sea of feudal darkness.

And wasn't, Naptha parried, Venice more a lesson of how the good fall into debasement, and wasn't Venice, then, with its dungeons and police spies the proper paradigm of man's rotten, spoiled nature, and didn't it further corroborate the evidence of man's fall from grace?

"That," Settembrini protested, "was when Venice had ceased to be herself, for she flourished without blemish well into the eighteenth century, evidence enough that other, yet greater societies might endure still longer. Civilization's lights were only recently sparked, a mere two thousand years."

An old argument, a stale apology: Venice spoke only for man's contemptible state, his vile and wormy lusts, man, man, man was shit, and, Naptha sputtered, Settembrini was shit, too.

"And," the Italian returned, "you, Naptha, are a spiteful, stunted crookback."

"A little arthritic in the shoulder, yes. That was God's work. But spiteful, no."

"Yes, spiteful," Settembrini said, "paying the world back for the hump of wrongs it so justly bequeathed you. Miserable *you* are, not man, but *you,* spewing bile on mankind's clean flesh."

"I'll have no more!" Peeperkorn bellowed. "This misrule I deem unfit for our friendly company. I enjoin you both to extend hands and clasp them in a show of goodwill and fellowship."

The combatants made wry faces and turned from the table.

"Apologize each," Clavdia said, "or I shall be very put out with you both."

"Very well, but I extend this hand under protest and because you, Madame Clavdia, have asked it," Settembrini said. "Infamy resides in that man, Signor Tintin, and it is better you know his true nature and let not yourself be corrupted by his lies. I shall place my hand atop his, but for an instant only."

"Watch, all," said Naptha, "for this meeting of hands shall happen so quickly as to seem never to have happened."

"Settled, then," Peeperkorn said. "And to settle all discontents, I enjoin you to join hands all. Let's ring this table

with a circle of hands entwined and let harmony reign where
discord once visited."

The circle of hands was formed over Naptha's and Settembrini's scowls and rumblings. In whose hand his left hand
resided Tintin did not know, so far away from him was his
hand on that side of his body; indeed, so distant from him
felt the whole of his body, except for his right hand, which
was now clasping Madame Clavdia's and which was receiv-
ing a gentle pressure from her source. Moments later, when
all had untied the knot of harmony ordered by Herr Peeperkorn, Tintin, embarrassed, found his hand still locked in
Madame Clavdia's in some bond whose name he did not
know.

—————— Chapter VIII ——————

[Dusk, the same day. Tintin and Clavdia are seated beside each other on a veranda facing the mountains and the darkening jungle. Clavdia clears her throat and begins to speak to the young man, whose flushed face is averted from her.]

"Well, Monsieur Tintin, from all that I have read, you are among the most active of... well, men, yet here you lounge about and seem of no apparent purpose."

"Yes, I do see your point," Tintin said laughingly. "But I've more than made up for my lack of motion with the terrible activity of my newly acquired mental life. I can scarcely sleep at night for all the ideas spinning in my weak head. How do you manage, Madame Clavdia?"

"To keep my head from spinning or how to keep an entire idea in my head? I'm not sure which you mean, but neither question is quite flattering. No, no, don't protest... I do fathom what you are saying. I was merely hunting for compliments—small game, to be sure—but yes, I have found a way, when the channel is too rough, as your companion the captain might say, to add some ballast to myself and make

the passage smoother. Your face, Monsieur Tintin, has such
a pretty glow, radiant of health, I assume.

"What were we saying?" Madame Chauchat asked. "Who
cares! Radiance, youth, the robust form! How wonderful.
How unlike the ideal of another time, when character and
charm and the quality of the mind counted for nearly all.
Personality, that was the thing! Personality is so wonderful.
When I was a child, no more than the age you have now,
my mother, her whole circle, in fact, spoke vividly of
personality as we do today of celebrity. My mother would
note of someone that he or she had personality or that some
other one lacked personality, and that would be all there
was to say. My father did not have personality, my mother
declared, and search as she might, she found that I did not
have it either. I tried to develop some, for it mortified me
to think I would go through life without it and to realize
that whatever exceptional thing I might do my mother
would not value it much or love me more than the halfway
love she gave me because, you see, I lacked personality,
and lacking it, I lacked the cause for love in others, for real
love, I mean. Affection, respect, tenderness, concern, none
of these did my mother deny me, and even until she grew
old and her eyes almost too feeble to cross a stitch, she
continued to knit sweaters for me and send them, in brown-
paper parcels tied with leftover old string, to wherever I
happened to be, even, as was once the case, in the tropics—
well, Belém is tropics enough for me, unless you consider
the sun steaming the river by seven in the morning not
tropics enough. It's uncanny how you devour words, Monsieur Tintin; you seem famished for them. Is there nothing
I have said you find dull? Oh, please don't do that with
your eyes; you make them so round I think they shall pop
out and roll away. Yes, that is better, thank you. I like

normal things and disdain oddities especially of the physical sort."

"You must find me very queer then, Madame Clavdia. I'm sorry if I disconcert you," Tintin said, his voice low, his eyes downcast.

"Somehow," Clavdia replied after a long pause, "I feel that I remember having answered you once before, long ago, in the same way that I shall answer you now: Forgive me, dear, sweet, young man for my thoughtless words. But I exclude you from my idea of the odd and have never considered you in such category from the moment my eyes contracted yours."

"Compacted mine? When was that?"

"That time, 'long ago and far away'—"

"When dreams were dreams of yesterday?"

"Yes, exactly. For today persons will believe anything, but rarely will they concede that love begins, is waiting for the love object long before the object is met . . . if it ever is to be met. That may or may not be the present case here, yet I do know that you do not depress me. For when I find myself in the company of ordinary, honest, good folk, I am not simply, as would be expected, bored. You must understand, Monsieur Tintin, as you will should our acquaintance ever ripen, that the company of ordinary people frightens and depresses me, the abyss, in short. To be with any less than the exceptional is a form of extinction. I feel pains in my chest, I grow dizzy with anxiety, with the thought that perhaps I will be condemned to the company of such as these for the rest of my life . . . 'these,' meaning, as you may gather, these human failures. Failure is worse than death, for death is final, but even in death there are traces that you have once lived. Failure, however, is extinction in the present, the never having lived, never having existed."

"I'm astonished, Madame Clavdia, and sad at the thought that anything can move you to unhappiness, you who require, indeed deserve, the buoyant and the famous!"

"How famous of you to notice exactly that! Yes. Let us once and for all admit that fame has its immense attractions. Only the superficial or those fearful of being thought snobs would deny that. The advantage of being famous is that you need not introduce or explain yourself to each stranger at a dinner party, for instance. When you are renowned, your mere presence is sufficient explanation for who and where you are . . . if you understand what I mean. But these are not thoughts that should, or indeed are intended to, occupy your mind, your being too young to be concerned with the foibles and insecurities of adults—especially of women past their magnetic moment—and famous enough never to feel the pains of anonymity. Ah!" Madame Chauchat continued, in a tone that signaled some profound disquiet, "there are rooms in one's life where one has spent stretches of misery so profound as to alter forever whatever pleasures daily life affords even the most fortunate, such as myself."

"It's strange, Madame Clavdia, how I have no idea of what you mean or what you are saying, yet I also know very well everything you are saying, know it from some distant and forgotten time in my life, but where could I have been and what was I doing then to give me so sharply this feeling of misery that you describe? Being small, holding the hand of some great grown-up while ambling along in their train on a Sunday afternoon when young and old strolled along in their Sunday clothes, then stopping off at some crowded café to take an ice or a pastry, and the waiting and waiting for the grown-up to decide to leave and take you home once again, where you are again alone, stiffly dressed for Sunday and sitting or standing in some grown-up's way—how they dislike you when they love you."

"I think you've got it. It's the boredom that I hated most."

"Yes, there is also that, but I'm speaking of the injustice of being a small one, of being tied to their dull lives—the lives of big ones, I mean. How many Sunday afternoons, with my Sunday clothes buttoned to my chin, did I long to be an Indian on the plains, to ride about on my great spotted pony and smoke a pipe at the campfire and stick my tomahawk into the head of some enemy brave?"

"Did you wear a long coat and shiny leather shoes?"

"A long blue coat and black shiny shoes. And since I always had a sore throat, I was made to wear a long red scarf, the scarlet color of my throat, Mother would say."

"Had I known you then, Tintin, I would have run off with you to the Americas or to the moon. Ah, if children only had the means, what different histories they would form of themselves!"

"How I would have protected you, Madame Clavdia, from wild animals and wild persons, in our skin-carpeted cave high in the mountain clouds, our nest hung with bear furs and antelope skins and illumined by a secret light of the sky. Yes, had we known each other then, we would have destroyed the vacancy of Sundays and the misery of being small."

"And what of the miseries of the present? Are there no aids for them?" Clavdia asked, her voice dropping. "Cannot grown-ups help their own kind to suffer less the dull shadow of the day?"

"Every person who knows you, madame, would help you to throw pails of brilliant light on this and every other mean shadow."

"Many have offered me the same, and yet when the moment of required aid arrives, the self-proclaimed assister rehearses other roles on other stages."

"I've been in the wings and sometimes in the orchestra and sometimes in a cozy box, and from these watches I have noted much villainy, but I have witnessed much kindness, too," Tintin said.

"Of course, all through this world are kind and bright persons, or there must be—so we all say. Yet when we are starting out anew in search for some intelligence and love, where are those sparkling, helpful persons? Men circle me when I'm least in need of them. But this subject grows gloomy! Let me blame this thin mountain air for lapsing into gloominess."

"Gloomy you shall not be. As long as there is life in me," Tintin exclaimed, his emphasis nearly tumbling him out of his chair.

"Well, my cavalier, you must remain on your mount should you wish to serve me," Clavdia chided mockingly. "Will you come, then, this evening, after dinner, to my room, where we may pursue further the service you volunteer?"

# Chapter IX

[That night. Clavdia's room. The moon bulging in the window.]

Tintin sits at the bed's edge, his arms folded, his thighs pressed tightly together. From a corner of her Hermès suitcase Clavdia Chauchat draws out a *bois des îles* casket, removing from it several glittering vials of crème de Java, oil of brazilwood, Amazon dew, essence of lilac, dragon's-tooth powder. These she mixes in a Chinese-blue porcelain bowl until they thicken into a smooth white cream.

"Tintin, undress!"

"Madame Chauchat!"

"Yes?"

"Clavdia!"

"Yes?"

"My clothes?"

"Yes, my darling boy, all."

Tintin slowly disrobes, leaving on, however, his blue boxer shorts.

"Now, my sweetheart, on your back. With the aid of this salve, I intend to elevate your spirits."

The Andean moon illuminates the room with its polished glow.

"This is more than I'd ever dreamed. More than life itself!" Tintin exclaims.

"Tintin," Clavdia whispers, kneeling beside the bed, "you are so strange, so hairless."

"I am a bit chilled, too."

"Indeed, you are," Clavdia answers, caressing the young man's chest.

Tintin sighs; his heart pounds; his face flushes; his skin tingles. Clavdia slowly draws down Tintin's boxer shorts, leaving them heaped about his ankles.

"Our night of love, finally."

"Our loving night, my beautiful Clavdia, my soul."

"You, a soul?"

"Soul-filled. Born by your touch."

"I feel, too, I've inspired yet another, more palpable growth."

"Your spirit has sparked the flesh."

*"Meno male."*

Long silence. Then chirps of crickets and the crackling of stones decomposing in the cold mountain night. Many sighs float to the ceiling, some breathed to the mattress. Faint odor of sea spray, roses, and honey. A blue glow emanates from bed center, where two animals collide and cohere.

"Ecstasy."

"Sublime."

"A new life. Should I die in the next moment, I would have no regrets, having lived so passionately in this interval."

"But, Tintin, I am only your first—"

"You shall be my only."

"Do not exaggerate. You are young, innocent, impressionable, generous. What do you know yet of sorrow, loss, of the dreadfulness of time? Do you know the icy wrenching, the salty burning of having to divide yourself from the one you love, and divide again until you are shorn and broken and lost? Do you know what it is to see the one you love fly from you, high and direct into the pure, free sky while you are left to remain and straggle earthbound, stranded on a desolate shore, left to age and to wither? We are alone, and always."

"But, Clavdia, you are too young, too loved to suffer these feelings."

"Adventure and novelty are all you understand, my sweet Tintin."

"I protest. You have awakened in me a capacity for love, too."

"Perhaps, but I cannot—I will not—allow it to be reserved for me. No matter, we have this night, and perhaps some few more days, here or elsewhere."

"I shall follow you."

"No, I sense your destiny is beyond you."

"I shall leave with you."

"To go where?"

"Anywhere!" Tintin exclaimed, his being flooded with a surge of images. "To Brazil, perhaps. To the moist green nights of Rio or Bahia, where I've never been. To hot sheets, and hotels, to sexlove and sexkiss and sexsigh and sexbreath to sex longings and sex spendings, and more."

"Oh! Tintin, your words compensate for your inexperience. But leave words now, and let's swim longer in the flowing wet of love."

"Clavdia, yes, but let's pause awhile to look at the moon."

"Yes, and we'll stay beside each other till the sun replaces her."

# Chapter X

Thus they fell asleep, side by side, smaller hand in larger, falling asleep at the same instant and beginning the same dream, their clasped hands the conducting link of the dream's mutual flow.

They were cantering across open plains, the red sun sliding slowly behind the snow-tipped peaks. At last glimpse of light, they came to a clump of cottonwoods beside a dark, swift creek, dismounted, and tethered their Arabian steeds. Tintin started a fire; Clavdia shot an antelope. While Tintin baked a lemon soufflé, Clavdia rolled fat cigarettes and laid out the bedrolls, saddles for pillows. At meal's end and with plates and utensils washed and stowed away, they smoked and played poker by the firelight, Clavdia winning most hands. The moon was up, full, pinned to the tree tips. Stars perforated the black sheet of heaven.

They had ridden hard for three days and had harder days yet before them. The plains would melt into hilly badlands and badlands level into burning desert. Dangers lay ahead. The outlaw Pimento and his pistoleros stood between them and the border, waiting to murder them, slowly. There were things with knives Pimento had sworn he would do to Tintin, while his men did other things to Clavdia before his sickened eyes. But for now they were safe, this night at least, under the cool draw of sky and the rushing whisper of creek. They played their cards and spoke and smoked.

Later, after checking and cleaning their weapons—Clavdia adjusting the hairwire trigger of Tintin's Colt six-shooter, he lining up the sights of her Winchester 77—Clavdia took out her guitar and sang a lonely song she had learned on the Argentine pampas or the Texas Panhandle.

> *Ayeee, ayeee, my lonely blood runs in rivers*
> *Ayeee, ayeee, get along, little dogies, 'fore*
> *my heart falls to betrayers . . .*

Then Tintin drew out his little accordion and sang a sea shanty he had learned at nights on the stormy Atlantic:

> *From stem to stern I'm your first mate*
> *So hey-ho, blow the man down . . .*

The songs and the singing and the tender flames of campfire biting into the night aroused them. Tintin unbuckled Clavdia's chaps and removed the spurs from her black, tooled boots. Clavdia undressed Tintin in turn. They grazed on each other. A jaguar watched from a short distance, marveling at the sight.

They broke camp at dawn, speeding out of the Badlands and into the high desert at the sun's hottest blaze, its flames grilling boulder and outcrop, braising earth and its stalkers large and small—lizards refrigerated under shale canopy, foxes slouched down in the miserly shade of cactus.

On the third day out, Tintin wasn't sure whether it was

the sun's effects on him or if he had really seen perched at a precipice's edge Pimento or, rather, his white beard peeking from behind a tree stump. Was the outlaw waiting for them to fall under the sun's blows before attacking?

Thirst-crazed, too weak to put up a good fight, they'd be captured without a scratch, but alive and well enough to suffer Pimento's cruel devices.

The day lengthened, shadows of mesquite and brush elongating into fantastic silhouette forms, a gondola cut through the sand, leaving a wake of blooming rosebushes, an Inca lord in full headdress played a huge guitar under a cantina umbrella, Snowy barked at a giant bemused bear; image after image rushed in a burning trail. Clavdia and Tintin staggered under the heat, their horses faltering in exhaustion. Water there was none, and shade neither. Tintin and Clavdia exchanged knowing looks—if they failed to cross the desert that night, they would be dead by the following day. They rode hand in hand so to protect each other from falling asleep and slipping off their mounts. But Tintin and Clavdia pretended it was love, not protectiveness, that linked them thus, and they began, with pitiful, strained voices, to sing:

> *Cross the prairie and the plain*
> *From the pampas to the north of Spain*
> *Hand in hand we'll ride together*
> *Cross the moor, desert, and the*
>     *heather.*

Tintin's palomino gave out first and with a great shudder died under him. They took turns riding and walking Clavdia's spotted pony until he, too, stumbled and fell, his mouth foamy, eyes glazed. Tintin shot him cleanly in the brain. Now both walked, arm in arm, stumbling, supporting each other, crawling on all fours, inching their way until they came to a ridge. Clavdia cried out; Tintin sighed in grief. Another desert lay before them, one flat and white, treeless, bushless, plantless, leafless, dry to the far horizon.

They had no strength to crawl their way over the vast stretch, even at night, and even if they had begun, they would be caught in the open expanse at daybreak and die there horribly in the day's full crushing heat. Death at least would cheat Pimento of his cruel pleasures.

They looked about them in the growing darkness. There at the end of the ridge appeared a fissure or crevice in the wall. When they reached it, they saw a narrow opening leading into a small cave. It went back several meters and ended where lay a pile of bones, some human, some of small animals.

"If we had water, I'd make us bone soup," Clavdia said, attempting to smile despite the pain of her parched lips.

"I hope we won't be left to that."

"You hate my soups, then. At last the truth."

They laughed.

"Make a broth of me," Tintin said lightly. "Sup on me till help arrives."

"Or you me. Should it come to that, darling," Clavdia answered softly, "I'm still the tastier here."

"Let's wait the limit for that solution," Tintin said, "though I'd rather it be I."

"Not I, Tintin. When we have to do it, let's do it at once and together."

"As with everything, Clavdia."

It was night, and the desert cold visited the cave. They stretched out, spent, sadness draping over them like wet clay. Tintin thought he'd wait for Clavdia to fall deeply into sleep and then, while she was still dreaming, shoot her in the brain and spare her the suffering ahead. And after, of course, a bullet for himself. Even in her sleep Clavdia was thinking his thoughts. Suddenly each spoke, saying the same words simultaneously: "No, not that way. I want to see you before going." They slept more easily with that reassurance.

Dawn's light filtered through the cave. Tintin felt the morning through his sleep. He felt, too, a cool wetness flicking about his face and hands. Presently, he imagined, he would dream of an oasis creek or a waterfall, of wonderful cascading water showering him and his drinking it. But no such dream arrived. He opened his eyes to find Snowy busy licking his hand.

Was it a dream? Snowy himself, frisky and juicy. Come from where? Tintin kissed Snowy's snout and eyes and buried his face on Snowy's neck.

"Good Snowy, my sweet lad. What a joy to see you!"

Tintin roused Clavdia to tell her of Snowy's mysterious arrival. Clavdia woke slowly, insensibly. Tintin saw in Clavdia's face and eyes the dehydration of her being, her cells shrinking, hardening, and dying.

She half smiled when she saw Snowy. "Is he real," she asked, "and is the captain here, too?"

"Alone, and real flesh and blood."

Snowy regarded the two with his head cocked. They seemed so drowsy, late to wake. *Get up, sleepyheads. Let's get going, lazybones.* He let out some snorts and a short bark but to little effect. Tintin merely raised himself on his elbows while Clavdia shut her eyes again. They were in a funk and best left alone for a while. He had plenty to keep him busy while they dallied. Bones. All kinds and sizes. A treasure of them. He went to the pile and rolled about the bone bed.

It wasn't Snowy back there rummaging among the bones but a dog that resembled him, a fake Snowy sent by Pimento to give them false hope and empty joy. To test him, Tintin ordered his return.

"Here, Snowy, come now!"

But the dog remained on his bed, gnawing on a fibula. Tintin called again, louder, and with the same results. Thundering figs! It was Snowy and not some terrier trained to deceive him, for Snowy was recalcitrant to any command, any pleading when it came to bones. How would Pimento have known that and trained the animal accordingly?

Good Snowy it was. Come from nowhere. But come for what? To die with them miserably in this foul cave. There flashed across Tintin's mind a dreadful thought, one so shameful that he winced and dug his nails into his palms to expel it.

Kill him. Eat him. Drink his blood. The thought would not go away. Tintin looked over to Clavdia. Burning she was, drying out. How long would she last without liquid? And how long Snowy himself? But to kill him! Tintin went back and forth on the matter. The image of a dead and devoured Snowy sickened him; the image of Clavdia suffering thirst and dying painfully also sickened him. Snowy's flesh might gain them some hours of life, and then who could tell what might turn up? A saving flood of rain, a caravan transporting red melons.

"Snowy," Tintin called out softly, "come."

Tintin's voice, with its gentle urgency, beckoned. *This is not an idle call,* Snowy thought, keeping the fibula clenched tightly in his jaw as he padded off to join Tintin. Tintin unholstered his pistol, keeping it in his hand as he stroked Snowy with the other. Clavdia woke and gazed up at the affectionate scene, feeling that for all its tenderness something terrible lay beneath it.

"Tintin," she cried, her voice more an accusation than a call. He turned, and their eyes met.

"No," she said, at the instant Tintin had come to the same word.

"Of course not. It was a lunatic moment, and it's passed. Off you go, Snowy, my boy."

Snowy scooted back to his treasure, pleased that Tintin had let him return to it without making more of a fuss. *He never wants me around these wonderful bones, shows me up for being too much dog, for his likes.*

What savagery and what a savage he was to think of hurting Snowy, of killing him, not to save his beloved dog from a gruesome death from hunger and thirst but so that he, Tintin, and Clavdia might live one day more. He had seen himself in the act, Snowy's limbs severed, his body gutted on the cave floor, while he with a mustache of blood and bloodied mouth and lips cracked the terrier's thighbone for its marrow.

An unfamiliar feeling of sorrow came over Tintin, a sorrow that actually burrowed beneath the layer of distress over their dreadful plight to a place in himself unknown. This new feeling gnawed at him the way Snowy was now gnawing at his bone, but there was no pleasure in these bitings and chewings into himself. And with these pangs now flowered a burning in his throat. How could anything burn more than this burning flower? Not even the sun waiting outside the cave. This feeling was what adults called remorse, guilt's punishment. This was why judges tried to determine whether a criminal felt remorse for the crime he had committed and why it was correct to soften the sentence for a criminal who felt it, for remorse was in itself a complete and harrowing punishment.

Tears flooded Tintin's eyes. Taking them for tears of sorrow for what awaited them all, Clavdia tried to console him.

"We have no regrets, have we? We've lived together more fully than most."

"And we have upset Pimento's plans," Tintin added lightly, determined not to let her know the new unhappiness visiting him lest it also visit her.

Snowy, too, had seen Tintin cry, a sight so unfamiliar that he dropped the bone from his jaw and let out a friendly bark. *Better stop playing with these bones and get to business.* He barked again, the bark Tintin recognized as Snowy's important call of discovery. Tintin made his way to the bone pile, where Snowy was now standing proudly, his tail rigid. Tintin could make out a narrow opening in the wall that the bone pile had concealed. Snowy took Tintin by his chaps to urge and lead him into the opening. Tintin slipped through to find a cool tunnellike chamber, its walls glowing faintly but with sufficient brightness to illuminate the room.

"Clavdia," Tintin called out, "I've found a passage where Snowy has come from."

*What did he think I was doing here if not come to rescue him, and how else did he imagine I had materialized?*

The tunnel went back farther than any limit Tintin could see. He returned to Clavdia's side and carried her into the tunnel. Snowy was far into the distance, beyond Tintin's vision, but he followed the sound of the terrier's barking for as long as his strength allowed. Pausing finally, he propped Clavdia against the glowing wall, which, as his hand passed over it, felt wet.

The walls were filmed with water, but not with enough flow to cup in a palm. Snowy returned to show Tintin the way, licking the wall with long slides of his tongue. Clavdia weakly followed suit.

Within some hours, they had regained enough strength to

follow Snowy deeper and deeper into the tunnel. Within some hours more, they felt the slightest of breezes caress their faces and they smelled the faint aroma of living things. When they became tired, they slept, Snowy curled between them. When they woke, they continued stumbling toward the endlessness of the tunnel and its eerie glow.

Tintin and Clavdia began to believe that the tunnel would lead them nowhere but to their deaths, that they would not have the strength to reach wherever it led and ended. But Snowy's cavorting, his sudden rushings ahead and racing back told Tintin that their goal was not too distant. Indeed, as the air suddenly freshened and snapped about them, they presently came to what seemed a thick bush or tree branch bathed in blazing light and blocking their path. Pushing aside the foliage, Tintin spied a green, sheep-dotted pasture before him. Sheepdogs darted about their woolly charges, while the immense sky busied itself with flocks of crows and burly white clouds. An observatory sat on a knoll, and below it gleamed a pond brimming with ducks. In the near distance, a huge house, its triple red chimneys piercing the slated mansard roof, its French windows gleaming and reflecting the golden light of the day and the blue tints of the vast ocean heaving before them.

They were home. Marlinspike.

In the following weeks Tintin and Clavdia stayed close within the manor, wanting to attend to matters of the estate after their long absence and to recuperate from their exhausting adventure. They breakfasted long and took long walks, returning to lunch and to ride again in the afternoon; they took tea and napped until dinnertime, when they dressed (Tintin in smoking jacket) and dined in the company of Captain Haddock and Snowy. The furrows in the captain's face had deepened; he had grown more portly. Snowy's gait had

slowed perceptibly, his whiskers gone soft. Distracted he had
become. In the middle of charging a pheasant he'd stop and
rush into a bush and fall asleep. "He's going stale," the captain
noted.

Tintin thought Snowy lacked companionship and brought
him a female snapped from the jaws of the local pound.
"Josie," read the name on her tag, and she answered to that
name, giving Tintin and Clavdia an appreciative snort and
jump whenever they called it. But Snowy was having no part
of her and ran from her to obscure niches of the house, where
he concealed himself. She was, Tintin finally observed, a
secret nipper, waiting to gain the confidence of man or fellow
dog only to sink her teeth into ankle or hind leg. Seeing the
impossibility of the relationship's developing further, Tintin
sent Josie to live in the workers' quarters.

One day Snowy disappeared in a driving rain. Tintin was
agitated all the while, fearing that his friend had been injured
in an accident or, worse, that Pimento or his henchmen had
kidnapped Snowy in lieu of his master and would return the
terrier to Marlinspike in a glass coffin, alive but mutilated.
With no success Tintin's agents scoured the countryside and
the cities, too, but just when all hope seemed lost, Snowy
reappeared with a companion in tow, a dog of Andalusian
origin, her name, Concetta, as pronounced by her platinum
tag. Now two dogs dined at evening table, their silver food
bowls set sometimes beside Tintin's chair, sometimes by the
captain's or Clavdia's. Peace again dwelled at Marlinspike.

One day while Tintin and Clavdia were out riding, they
noticed a new shepherd tending their flock. Familiar he was,
not so much in his face, which was grizzled and the color of
lightly grilled salmon, but in his straight posture and huge
frame. They rode closer, finding to their alarm that the shepherd under his hood was their long-sworn enemy Pimento.

Tintin drew his pistol, forgetting that he wore none. The old outlaw pulled aside his cloak. Tintin, thinking that his enemy was about to draw, hurled himself before Clavdia. But no shot rang out, no fierce oath and curse issued from the outlaw's lips. Instead a small, supplicating voice came from beneath the shepherd's cowl.

"I've not come to harm you but to ask your forgiveness for the ill I've done you in the past."

He was actually kneeling, this ancient foe.

Clavdia and Tintin looked about them to see where the outlaw's men were hiding, sure that the old man's plaint was merely a ruse. But there was no one in the area but the red sheep and Josie, the dog working the flock.

They took the shepherd, Pimento, back to the house, where, over scotch and dark soda, they heard his tale. It was while waiting to capture them at the border—by what miracle they had escaped him he did not know—there in the highlands of Peru, those many years ago, that a jaguar had seized him and made him prisoner. But instead of devouring him, the jaguar made him promise to give up his lust for revenge against them and to lay down his weapons and turn toward a tamer life. This he promised, never intending to keep his word.

And no sooner was he released from the cat's paws than he went again to his old life of lies and lechery, of subterfuge and pilfering, of aesthetic sabotage. Then, one day, while he was crossing Chapultepec Park in Mexico City, on his way to Chicago, there in the middle of the path in the broadest of broad days, a day wide and bright and full of sky, the jaguar reappeared.

"I'll not kill you, liar. But punishment there is," the jaguar declared. And with those words the jaguar leaped into a tree and vanished, the last objects living or inanimate the forsworn one would ever see again, for he, the jaunty old Pimento, had gone forever blind.

Years of wandering ensued. Begging alms, doing an occasional odd job, raging to no avail against the darkness and his enemies, and generally exhausting himself in misspent anger. Repentance was at hand, however, the renunciation of all his vile acts and vices followed, and sweetness took the place of bitterness, light filled him. He was a changed man.

"How is it that you are tending sheep when you are blind?" Clavdia asked suspiciously.

That was the beauty part. The more he changed, the better his vision, his sight being slowly restored to him with every good deed and thought, and now he was waiting here at Marlinspike, to beg their forgiveness in hope that the final veil would be lifted from his eyes.

"Forgiveness and more," cried Tintin, conducting the reformed person to the manor doors. Pimento would be made the first shepherd, and when he was no longer able to perform his pastoral services, he would have a place in the kitchen by the stoves, where he would always be warm in the winter or summer. No sooner was Pimento installed in the quarters closest to the manor house than Clavdia, feeling the strangest aches and pains, gave birth to a son, a blond child with a blond cowlick and the suggestion of a white beard, whom they named Little Tintin. Later in the day, Concetta presented Snowy and their human friends with a son, a pure terrier, whom Tintin named Little Snowy. Captain Haddock announced he would be Little Tintin's godfather and watch over him, and Pimento voted himself the same for Little Snowy. Then, to celebrate the event, the captain downed several glasses of cheer, tucked himself away in the northwest wing of the manor in the large, open room where the ospreys had set up their tall nests. Pimento immediately went about teach-

ing Little Snowy how to retrieve purses and wallets flung to
the farthest reaches of the main hall. Clavdia flew to Paris to
buy a new wardrobe now that her body had resumed its
fabulous shape. Once there she met friends and stayed two
weeks longer than expected. Little Tintin rang her up at the
hotel because of problems he was having translating some
passages from Ovid; he was certain that those passages would
be on his university exams, and he asked her, in passing,
whether it was usual for women his age to carry pistols and
little red books in their handbags, because he had met one,
called May, who did and who was perfectly earnest and very
pretty.

When Clavdia returned, hatbox filled with gloves and exhibition catalogs, she found Tintin at his desk, still writing
his memoirs. They kissed, Tintin enchanted by the aroma of
her new perfume, by the saucy cut of her hair, by her smooth,
waxed legs. She admired the intellectual look his bifocals gave
him, the red rims of his eyes fatigued from reading and writing, the slight scholarly slope of his shoulders as he bent to
kiss her again. Little Snowy came into the room while they
were making love. So grown he had become that Tintin
wasn't sure whether it was Snowy father or son that had
come into the room, having forgotten for a moment that the
father had died quietly in his arms one spring morning, his
grave beside Concetta's. Wheeled there by the new chauffeur,
Captain Haddock often spent time by their graves, thinking
his thoughts cold sober, for he had long given up the bottle.
Sitting in his wheelchair, rug over his inert legs, the captain
mused on the nature of his love for Snowy, deeming it more
than his love for all but Tintin. He regretted he had never
told Snowy that.

The new chauffeur, Herr Napberg, was impatient with
these grave visits, claiming that his services did not include

the transporting of passengers in their wheelchairs.

"Take the gardener's job then," Tintin suggested. "You won't have to stir except among pots and plants."

The chauffeur would not hear of it. "The people of my race do not till land. We traverse giant space with engines and motors, not furrow baby hectares with plow and hoe."

How familiar he was, this Herr Napberg, with his certainties and insistent voice. A voice from the far past, when conversation ran riot and tempers burst, the hungry days, when ideas were more wanted fare than food on the table.

Now Tintin went to appeal to the most recently hired gardener, tracking him down to a remote section of the estate where tomatoes of several varieties were planted in season, Tintin enjoying especially the sweet plum tomatoes, which he harvested and ate all through the month of August. There he found the man busy tying plants to stakes and oblivious of the sounds of his approach. The gardener was singing or speaking to himself—or to his leafy wards—in the purest Tuscan tones: " *'Vedi Parìs, Tristano; e più di mille ombre mostrommi e nominommi a dito, ch'amor di nostra vita dipartille.'* "

Tintin ventured a discreet cough and called out the gardener's name: "Signor Settembroglio." His interruption jarred the melodious intoner and even seemed to disquiet the flowering plants whose erect, firm leaves now appeared to droop beside their stakes.

"*Guarda!* You have stricken me and my charges with your sudden manifestation. See how they tremble, my children. Gentleness, sir, the soft tread and softer voice, or how else are we to grow into the forms destined us?"

Tintin politely apologized for his indiscretion and went to the matter at hand, impressed, nonetheless, by the gardener's admonitions. But the gardener, as did the chauffeur before him, refused the task. No, he was no walker of old sea dogs or of any manner of dogs, the gardens and their growths being his province, as he had long ago decided that it was wiser and more rewarding to tend to the needs of flora than to those of humans.

"Very wise, indeed, sir," Tintin said respectfully. "I see you are a bit of a thinker. Much like Herr Napberg, the chauffeur who came here the week you arrived, I think."

"I'm acquainted with no such person," the gardener said with a dismissive gesture. "My thoughts do not notice persons any longer."

The matter concluded there, though the gardener did explain, and at great length, the estate's need for an orchard of pears and figs and for a patch of basil for his own use. Tintin limped away, walking slowly on his good leg and weighing heavily down on his stout oak cane—Clavdia's gift. He would wheel the captain himself and rely on no one in these matters of sentiment—a reflection on life in general that he would note in his memoirs immediately. He searched about the house for Clavdia to tell her of his encounters with the gardener and chauffeur, of how they reminded him of the two intellectual antagonists they knew those many years ago on that strange Inca mountain in Peru. But Clavdia was nowhere on the premises, and none of the servants had seen her since breakfast.

Tintin went to his study to resume writing his memoirs. Scarcely had he touched pen to page when he heard a loud boom and thud. From the window he could see that out there in the ancient park an ancient oak had jumped its roots and lay on its side, branches flailing. Already some of his staff had rushed out to see the beached giant; Clavdia was there, too, and Pimento beside her, and Little Snowy was inspecting roots and trunk and letting out short howls. Tintin wanted to go down to join them, but he felt exhausted. He would learn about the tree later. How could he leave when he had so much more to write! He was still in the early years, before Machu Picchu, before Clavdia had given grace to his life. He had so much more life to cover that he thought his task would never end. Little Tintin could resume where his father had left off, but the boy's interests were elsewhere, in the direction of electrifying the world with his plans for raising dams and power stations the planet over, to bring light to jungle and cave, desert and tundra. An engineer he had become, this lad, with not too much concern for the reflective life, just as he himself had been at his son's age.

Tintin realized that he had been writing without his bifocals on—no wonder his tiredness—and he searched about the room to find them. Nothing. He went downstairs and rummaged through the kitchen, then on to the library, and from there to the hothouse, where he had been grafting roses that morning. Moans, sighs, and voices came from the tomato bed, where Clavdia was lying, blouse open, tartan skirt folded above her thighs, her wig askew. Beside her groaned Pimento, shirtless, and beside him his broken and splintered shepherd's crook.

"Rapture. Quite. Amazing. As always. Suffice to say no more. My dear."

Still without his bifocals, Tintin returned to his study and sat himself down in a large leather chair. His head reeled; his heart sank to its lowest basement. He was thinking miserable thoughts when Clavdia came to find him. She stood behind him, clasping his eyes with her hands. She loved him, would always. But a part of their lives together had terminated, and now there would be slight changes. She would be spending some of her nights with Pimento, some with him, and some alone. And unless Pimento was away in town, he would be dining with Tintin and her most evenings. She tenderly kissed Tintin's forehead and started to leave the room.

Tintin's voice arrested her. "Could he have plotted a better revenge, Clavdia?"

Now he was alone again. Little Snowy came to him often and stayed near his bed on nights when Tintin slept solo, but Tintin did not find in the son the father's loyal affection. Little Snowy, born to a generation of comfort and adventuresomeless, had not swum rivers nor slid down cliffs nor faced all manner of death by his master's side. All bones were the same to him, those on his plate as juicy as those won from a deep ditch or wrested in a fight. He was a house dog, kind, present, but with a limit to his understanding of the intensities and shades of Tintin's moods and needs.

So when he stayed beside his lonely master, Tintin did not feel less lonely by much, except insofar as Little Snowy reminded him of the other Snowy, life's veteran.

Captain Haddock was of little help as well. He had become forgetful in sobriety, or as he once lucidly remarked, he had become sober just when drinking cheated him of memory. On those rare nights at dinner with Tintin Clavdia Pimento he would lurch forward after a long silence and, pointing to the former brigand, ask, "Who's this lubber?" He asked the same when pointing to Clavdia. At times the captain did not remember where or at what moment of his life he was living. Tintin noticed that the captain stashed food and especially bread away in his greatcoat while dinner was in progress and later learned that the old seaman thought he was still the hungry young swab hoarding sugar cubes and hardtack to consume on late watch.

Once, in the middle of dessert, he attacked Pimento with a carving knife he had tucked away in his belt. "Avast! Pirates larboard. Repel boarders," he shouted, lunging at the surprised man's throat, just as some lemon sherbet was coolly passing down it.

The blade missed but had come close enough to the mark to alarm its target, although the deed itself was sufficient to create a stir. In the days to come Pimento demanded that the captain be sent away; he himself had found a snug place, a retired seamen's home called Sailor's Cove located in the Swiss mountains. Clavdia reluctantly joined in the petition. It was for the captain's own safety, she said, for soon he would do injury to himself as well as others, and he needed more tending than the household staff and Tintin himself was capable. No matter how much they pressed, Tintin remained firm. And finally it was decided that Pimento and Clavdia would take their meals without the captain and leave Tintin to join them or not as he pleased.

Now Clavdia came to him less often, and when she did, she was at war with herself and consequently with him. She came late in the evening, after Tintin, despairing of her company, had finally gone to sleep. She would slip into the room quietly and slide under the covers silently and remain still, hoping he did not notice her entry and would be satisfied, on his waking, simply to find her there. But for all her calculations, once asleep, Clavdia was unable to maintain her aplomb and cried out his name from the depths of her dreams, and sometimes she unconsciously reached out to him, pressing herself against him, he who smelled of milled wheat and blond honey.

Small satisfactions arrived unexpectedly and soured quickly. Little Tintin arrived one day with a wife in hand. Tintin and Clavdia were happy to see their son settled, given over to conjugal pursuits. But they soon learned that while he had intended to travel no longer and plant himself and family (two of the children would visit Marlinspike over the next school holidays) firmly at home, he had plans for the reconstruction of Marlinspike itself. It was too large, too expensive, too feudal. "Too elitist," May, his wife, added. They would break up the huge manor and divide the rooms into convenient housing units for hundreds. Of course, anyone could do that, it took no special talent to imagine such worthy renovations, but—and here was the great novelty— Little Tintin would flood the estate with seawater and dam it to produce power and electricity by utilizing the ocean's tides.

Thus the Marlinspike compound would be self-sufficient from the energy standpoint and serve as a model of efficiency to the world. There were even additional advantages. Whatever excess power the station generated would be sold at reasonable rates to surrounding parts of the country, ensuring a modest profit above that derived from rents. These profits would prove indispensable at a time when costs of education and of educating Tintin's and Clavdia's grandchildren were mounting. Not to speak, offered May, of the huge expense of clothing two teenagers, of the costs of insurance for their cars and the money needed for their summer holidays.

Admirable in its outline, most especially the part dealing with the nonpolluting use of sea power to create energy, the plan did not take into account certain factors, Tintin and Clavdia replied. For one, there was the issue of Marlinspike's present tenants, not to mention the shepherds, gardeners, chauffeur, cooks, house servants, and all those others whose livelihood derived from the well-being of the estate. Then there was the matter of the land itself, its orchards, tomato and basil patches, hills, and trees—some very ancient—its English gardens, and mysterious alleys of French hedges so carefully tended, and the livestock, where would they go?

All under the sea. And what of the nonfunctional value, the elusive matter of beauty? Was not Marlinspike a work of beauty, and did it not give consolation and serenity to all those who knew and who in generations to come would know it?

A vast park open to all was what Tintin and Clavdia had planned for Marlinspike after their deaths. For the present, Little Tintin had vast sums in his own fund; he wouldn't even have to dip into principle to live at the highest level. As for the future, Little Tintin and his family would be richly provided for in Tintin's and Clavdia's wills, and as for money for the children, why, there was plenty to be had for the asking. Ask.

Having money was not the same, Little Tintin rejoined heatedly, as putting his plans to effect in his own country, the first in the world to have such a complex of sea power and housing.

"Father"—Tintin recoiled from the unfamiliarity of the appellation applied to him—"I shall not be impeded. I shall take the matter to the courts, if need be."

The courts and their battles, words hurled in an official room, humans pinpricked by words and bled to a slow and expensive death.

Where were the sandy dunes he had crossed on thirsty camel, where the oceans he had sailed on ship and shipwreck's raft, where the prairies he had ridden and the sky he had slept under, where the intricate networks of criminals' tunnels and caves under unsuspecting cities he had traversed, where the craggy islands and brooding castles he had explored, where all his explorations and exploits now but winnowed down to acrimony over property? The blows were coming from everywhere and from everywhere closest to him, better the jungle with its claws and poisonous stings than this.

The matter was still unresolved when Little Tintin and May sped away in their car. A long drive through the countryside and a stop at the local pub and café for a pint and a glass of calvados, that would clear his head and temper his injured heart, Tintin thought, making his way to the garage.

The garage doors were already open. From within came loud banging noises, shouts and cries. Stepping inside, Tintin saw two men dueling. The chauffeur, armed with a tire iron, and the gardener, equipped with a short rake, lunged and parried and beat their weapons against each other, iron bar clanging against iron tines. Each had been struck, for blood ranged down their faces and covered their hands, and cries of their pain mixed with curses and threats.

"*Bestia!* I break open your face."

"*Schweinehund!* I twist out your eyes."

Tintin shouted for them to halt, and they did immediately, more in surprise at seeing their employer than for their wish to obey him.

"This time we finish everything once and for all," the chauffeur said.

"An end to his infamy and lies," countered the gardener.

Tintin pleaded with them to put down their weapons and discuss the issues infuriating them.

"Never! We've talked enough."

"We've said everything already."

"Then I fire you both here and now," Tintin said.

"Who cares a fig, so long as the other dies," the gardener said.

"Yes, fire me and watch how death resigns him," the chauffeur added.

They picked up their weapons and charged each other with renewed vigor. Tintin tried to place himself between the two, but they would allow nothing to interrupt their fury, saying they would join together to fight him rather than terminate the battle with each other. To make their point yet clearer, the combatants brandished their weapons in Tintin's face.

"All right," Tintin said finally, "let be what is. Either calm yourselves or slaughter each other, but end it here, for I have no wish to see either of you again." (Not true his ultimatum, for he knew he would always want to see them, have them enlarge his mind, his perspectives and views.)

He had hardly finished his words when the two, with fiendish grins, resumed the attack.

Tintin retreated to the manor house, thinking to tell Clavdia about the mad pair in the garage, whom he had finally recognized as Naptha and Settembrini in disguise, but he remembered, painfully, that Clavdia had left him some while ago to live with Peeperkorn, who, discarding the pseudonym Pimento, had retaken his former name. Perhaps it was the bloody scene he had just witnessed that inspired the impulse, for now Tintin thought of bloodletting and murder, too. He would go down to the city and kill Peeperkorn and rid himself of him once and forever and reclaim Clavdia once and forever. Why had he not thought of it before? Why had he waited so long to have the thought visit him and to admit its entry?

Cowardice, perhaps. No, not that. He had faced death openly many times and would still beard it, but it was easier to die than to kill, and he had never killed before, not even in self-defense. But he would now, in spite of all the injunctions against it, in spite of all the horror he felt in doing it, for Peeperkorn-Pimento had not merely threatened his life— he had threatened it many times in the past—but he had robbed him of half his soul, the Clavdia share, without which now he was truly dying before his death.

A wonderful rage was in him and would cease only when its object had been smashed, not killed, simply, but made broken and bleeding, head split open, brains steaming on the tile or sinking in the carpet. Violent death, pounding and painful death, teeth kicked out of the head, internal organs bruised and anguished death. Nothing less would do now. Tintin found his old pistol and a small blackjack the captain used to carry when they went prowling among wharves at midnight. A small, hand-size thing it was, black leather covering a lead sinker, the braided handle hard and pliant, quick to strike; it could snap a man's head open as if it were a chicken's egg.

He knew where to find them; they had left him an address, dismissing in that gesture all sense of his being a threat. But what was meant for his humiliation was now their danger. He would relish the surprise on their faces when he appeared, pistol in one hand, snapper in the other.

Not a word, no recriminations or denouncements, no trying to wring fear and remorse from them, just a bullet or two for Peeperkorn, in his guts, to subdue him; then he'd let the blackjack do the remaining brutal, crunching work.

A Georgian house, naturally. Clavdia's choice, of course. Her taste ran to that, Georgian silver, Georgian tea service, Georgian furniture, Georgian portraiture. Unlike him, Clavdia shunned the Second Empire in all its physical forms and would not allow a stick from that period into their home. Not that he himself was so much in love with Second Empire—but that was another matter. What would he do with Clavdia, now that he was here, standing before this Georgian house? Not kill her, no. Wither her with coldness? Not effective; she would merely grow colder. Rage against her and blame her for the mayhem she had caused (pointing at all times to the battered mess that was once Peeperkorn)? She would merely grow sleepy, rage being her narcoleptic trigger.

The door opened. A woman in livery addressed him.

"You must be Monsieur Tintin, is that you?"

Tintin nodded.

"Yes, Madame Clavdia thought she spied you through the window just now. Madame Clavdia waits for you upstairs."

The woman conducted Tintin to the doorway of the bedroom. Clavdia rose from the seat beside the huge bed where Peeperkorn lay wheezing, mouth open, hand on his chest.

"How did you know to come?" Clavdia asked with wild glee.

The man in bed made choked noises, his head jerking spasmodically.

"He's too weak to speak now, but he understands everything, Tintin, my love."

Clavdia rushed to Tintin's side, took his face in her hands, kissed him.

"Clavdia!" Tintin exclaimed, drawing back from her, pistol sighted toward Peeperkorn.

"No, Tintin, don't you see he's dying?"

"No matter," Tintin said dreamily, "I still need to destroy him." He returned the revolver to his pocket and drew out the blackjack from the other.

"I've done that for us," Clavdia cried. "I've been poisoning him forever, and now he's finished. His muscles and nerves are paralyzed; his windpipe's constricting. Look at his face: He can't breathe, he's strangling."

Clavdia sat at the edge of the dying man's bed and motioned for Tintin to sit beside her and witness Peeperkorn's last pain-filled minutes. "He'll go blue, then purple," she said, half laughing, half pitched to hysteria, "and then he'll go to hell."

(Blue to purple, yes, he'd splash some bruised purple on Pimento's face with his snapper, a whack and a thwack across the cheeks and a little something between the eyes.)

Clavdia shuddered and cried long, tear-pearls until Tintin held and calmed her. Thus comforted, she was eager to unfold her tale. Her tale: No sooner had Pimento come into the household under his contrite persona than he threatened to kill Tintin and every living person and thing related to the estate, sheep, horses, dogs, flowers, orchards, the captain, Tintin's son—in short, to murder their world. She thought he was both mad and bluffing, but he explained to her how he had mined the manor house and the dwellings on the estate so that at his will the all of it would blast into flaming splinters, and he had mined, too, the dams and causeways to the sea so that the great salt ocean would rush and flood the land and with its great wet saltiness forever kill the earth and its lovely pear trees and rose beds and basil patches and drown duck, lamb, sheep, walking mutton, kid, and kine and drown again all creatures walking or crawling atop or inching below the land down to the last bug and worm.

To prove his power, Pimento exploded the roots of a huge oak in the park beneath Tintin's study window—did Tintin remember that tree, the noble one that grew there before Columbus ever crossed the gangplank to the Americas?—and promised that unless she slept with him that hour, he'd blow Marlinspike to the clouds. And so she did, and so, too, did his demands increase each passing day. (She was asked things too loathsome for the telling, things a gentleman such as Tintin would never have dreamed!) She accommodated and waited, waited for the time when she would be in position to find the former brigand and faux shepherd vulnerable, acceding slowly to each and every demand, suffering the thought of how Tintin was hating her and was suffering, too. Finally she maneuvered Pimento out of Marlinspike and into the present domain, where he believed he could control her completely and dominate all future prospects with the high card of his threat. But she planned otherwise. She took with her a vial of poison, a potent nerve paralyzer and life suffo-cater, a souvenir of her and Tintin's Amazon expedition, when they lived among the Xingú river people, and fed the poison to him in minute fractions of droplets ever so slowly over months and years until he became the present wreck in the bed. Of course, Pimento was suspicious of his failing health, watched her for signs of her doing exactly the mischief she was in fact doing, but finding no indications of her com-plicity in his waning powers, he became a devotee of the doctor's office, dragging himself and her along with him to one medical examination after another.

His blood and urine tests showed nothing to indicate he was being slowly poisoned—such was the virtue of this mag-nificent, subtle, and occult substance—showed only that he was, along with the rest his age, growing old and subject to the numbing, debilitating infirmities of his human kind.

The history of his medical adventures would make quite a story in itself, if one had the time to recount it and could find an auditor sufficiently interested, but an aspect of it might appeal to Tintin. His patience worn out by the normal and dead-end routes of Western medical science, Pimento tried the East, becoming the patient of a Chinese doctor of great obscurity and Mandarin presence whose herbs, roots, pow-dered deer antlers, smelly brackish brews, and gleaming acu-puncture needles seemed actually, and from her standpoint disastrously so, to improve the sick man's condition. But the doctor left the country and his small windowless office just when Pimento seemed most in remission from his aches and creaks, his disorienting fatigues, all of which returned to him in greater than ever force once the Chinaman had departed.

Wheezing and gasps interrupted Clavdia's account. Pimento, she noted, was in condition blue and would shortly proceed to the purple, the color that portended his final round.

For the moment, Tintin hardly noticed Pimento's coloration, so struck was he by Clavdia's loquacious narrative and its meanderings or rather by Clavdia's remarkable, discursive, newly found, rotund voice. Had she lain with the master of words for so long that she now spoke with his tongue? No matter, now it was the master himself who needed attending to, the deadly blush of plumpurple glowing on his otherwise immobile face.

"Clavdia," Tintin said, "we can't let this go further."

"Do you wish that I give him the antidote and restore him to life so that he can rejuvenate his actions against us? And perhaps succeed where last he failed?"

Of course, not that, but they could not let him die this way either. They had never taken a life before, and this burden for their freedom from Pimento would be too crushing to bear. They continued this exchange until at last they hit upon a scheme.

Clavdia injected a clear white liquid into Pimento's arm that had the effect of returning his complexion to blue, then to a faint pale egg-white blue, then within the hour to its normal florid color. The spreading poison had been halted, and some of its effects had been reversed but not to the point where all of Pimento's functions had returned or would ever return. And thus they brought him back to Marlinspike, a large man with a white beard unable to speak or walk, unable to move all but his head, and that ever so slightly. He lived in a wheelchair or sometimes remained merely propped up on some divan or chaise longue in some foreign part of the manor.

Little Snowy enjoyed looking at the immobilized creature

and would stare at him for hours, an occupation that left Tintin wondering at the dog's intelligence, though he would not allow himself to believe that in the transition from one generation of dog to another anything at all had been altered. So much of the old life had changed at Marlinspike that in desperation to maintain the illusion that little had changed, Tintin pretended Little Snowy was in fact Snowy *père* and would talk to him about events and adventures that occurred before the junior dog was born. Among other fictions Tintin promulgated, one concerned the former gardener and chauffeur, both of whom had vanished before the reunited couple returned to their conjugal life *chez* Marlinspike. The garage where Tintin had last seen the combatants was left in pristine state: Waxed and polished cars gleamed as new; spare tires stood straight in their racks; wrenches and tools were aligned in perfect order along the workbench wall. Only one blemish marred the spotless scene. The concrete floor where the two antagonists had battled was blotched by a hand-size reddish stain, which remained stained after several vigorous washings. Finally Tintin had the garage floor painted marine blue, making the cars appear to be floating in a grotto pool.

Either one had killed the other and had removed himself and the corpse from the premises or both had left to live or to fight elsewhere or to die elsewhere. Wherever they were, he missed them. Although they had long been replaced—a Japanese man with wife and children supervised the gardens (banishing from them basil, eggplant, and peppers), and a Brazilian from Belém, who drove at breathtaking speeds heedless of Madame's gasps and cries, took over the wheel or the wheels—Tintin spoke of the absent antagonists as if they were still present and still functioning in their respective positions.

"I see Signor Settembroglio's put up daffodils this year, very good that line of buttery yellow along the green hedge path."

"I'll tell him you're pleased," Clavdia replied, humoring him, as she lately had grown accustomed to doing.

One day Tintin handed Clavdia a copy of Nietzsche's *Beyond Good and Evil,* asking her to return it to its owner. "Very instructive, eye-opening that book. Please tell Herr Napberg how much I enjoyed it—enlarges the mind, you know."

Clavdia simply brought the book to the house library, where she placed it on the shelf among the other returned-to-their-owner books she presumed he also never had read. But Tintin was unpredictable in matters of change. While he would brook no truth in the matter of the vanished gardener and chauffeur, he made no denial of Captain Haddock's death.

Still bound to his wheelchair, the captain one day seemed to have his faculties returned to him. He no longer referred to Clavdia as "that lubber," and he came to recognize Pimento even in his mummified state, though he did from time to time prod the immobilized man with his cane, calling him "ballast" and "bilgepie" and "pirate cheese." He had come to his senses at last, the captain said, and he was now going to write his memoirs. Tintin reminded him of the great difficulty in ever finishing them—as he himself was evidence— or of even ever getting to the crucial parts and rendering them satisfactorily. Nothing dissuaded Haddock, and he went to his room after meals and devoted himself to writing.

It was curious, Clavdia noted, that men and women who had moved about so much in their lives one day, out of the blue, felt the need to immobilize themselves in the most cramped positions and scratch out words about the invisible past. She was happy thinking about the happy parts and forgetting the rest, and even at that, she was happiest thinking of nothing at all but the present, the only time, actually, that existed.

Haddock concurred with the justice of her remarks, adding, however, that while he was writing, he was in a sort of motion, most so when he was most fixed, a state of fixed motion. He seemed to delight in this state so much that he stayed in his room longer and longer intervals, much to Tintin's amazement and envy. Curiosity often brought Tintin to Haddock's door. There he stood and listened. The long silences were sometimes broken by exclamations—"Trim sail!" and "Clear way"—and once Tintin heard a long howl, "Drown me in a squall."

One day when Haddock seemed to be working away unusually long, Tintin sent up a late lunch, the captain having grown increasingly unmindful of meal hours. But when the meal and servant returned, Tintin grew alarmed. The captain had not responded to the servant's knock and call, not even to berate him for the interruption. Tintin knew Captain Haddock was dead, and indeed, he was dead and still at his post, pen in hand, slumped over the logbooks in which he had written not his life's story but Tintin's.

The captain had brought the narrative well beyond the place where Tintin had left his off but still short of finishing the adventure in Machu Picchu. He told of how he and Tintin had first met that terrible time when he was drinking and had lost the crew's respect and how unscrupulous officers had plotted to keep him drunk and quartered in his cabin so he would not notice the drug traffic they were conducting with and on his ship. Besotted he was, unaware of how he was being used, and happy to have others do his job, leaving them to run the ship and his life, too, as long as the whiskey was brought to his cabin and flowed to his mess. It was then that Tintin appeared, this strange, indefatigable boy, one night, secretly boarding the ship to search for evidence of illegal cargo. Tintin found the drugs, and discovered Haddock, too, drunk in his cabin and lost to the world. Tintin sobered him up and apprised him of the ship's doings and gave him a chance to win back his loyal crew and rid the ship of its criminal usurpers.

From that day onward he was at Tintin's side, perhaps not always sober but clearheaded enough and in charge of himself. The rest of the narrative told of Tintin's adventures the world over and told them in a voice sweet, economical, and assured. Tintin could hardly take himself away from reading the logbooks, forcing himself to put them down briefly on the morning the captain was interred in a plot beside Snowy's. It was only several days after the captain was in the ground that Tintin read a passage in the logbooks outlining the seaman's desires on the matter of the disposal of his mortal remains.

The instructions—for that is what Tintin took them to be—were couched in the form of a wish. Would that the narrator meet the fate of his seagoing ancestors and be placed with his instruments of his profession, his sextant, compass, and spyglass, in a craft of navigable size—larger than a dinghy and smaller than a schooner—and set aflame out at sea so that he and craft would burn to ash and marry with billow and brine. He would then not be so much in the sea but of it. Atoms of him flung on shores, his misty spume racked across the sunbeams of morning, atoms of him in the lungs of whales and in the tissue of fishes. He'd swim with and tack against the tides, plunge to the blackest bottom of the sea only to climb up again on backs of dolphins gliding to the brilliant day.

Tintin had the captain's body disinterred and followed the

dead man's wishes. From his study window Tintin saw the yawl bob out to the horizon and flare into fire like a red match on a plate of sudsy water. Then the flame sputtered out, and with it the last of the earthbound Haddock.

Tintin left the captain's grave and headstone intact, though nothing lay beneath it except the memory of Haddock's brief stay there.

Clavdia was all Tintin had left of the old life, and he hers. His grandchildren visited infrequently, his son and daughter-in-law never. Little Snowy's offspring roamed about the estate half wild, a threat to the sheep. Little Snowy had grown too old to have control over them, and their poodle mother offered no direction, having abandoned husband and children to follow a life with a black Labrador whose roots were in the city. Parentless, ill mannered, and savage, they were pampered by Tintin, who saw in their eyes the glimpse of their grandparents, of Snowy.

Memories of former days and attention to the few demands of the household kept Tintin little occupied. To see Tintin puttering about the house in ever-widening circles of distraction saddened Clavdia, she herself filled with projects and activities each day and week. As a former explorer, world traveler, racing car champion, rose garden expert, she was in demand to give lectures and organize charity parties. She was famous and sought after. In old age one must be wanted and rich, she would say. The former, because to be shunted by the roadside is to feel the isolation of the deep grave before the grave's call, and the latter because independence and options grow from the soil of cash, and where there is cash there is currency.

Tintin had long given up writing his memoirs and had little by way of activities to challenge him. Clavdia tried to get him on the lecture circuit, but he was a resolute failure on the platform. Where in life he was natural and graceful, his style and carriage plain, on the stage mannerisms invaded his gestures, shrugs of shoulders, waves of the hand or, when he thought the occasion demanded, both hands; he waxed rhetorical, lowering his voice and making the most artificial pauses to signal that something momentous was to follow. These and other embellishments ruined his image. The public who had read of him and his adventures and who had come prepared to see a stout, artless man found standing in his place a ham. So the stage was out, and he returned to his puttering and reading the mail, which he had come more and more to expect and depend on, waiting at the window in pajama and robe for the postman to arrive before dressing for breakfast. One day the post brought a rich travel brochure in the wake of letters soliciting money and his signature. Travel, the once-dangerous, adventure-ridden, and consuming occupation of his and Clavdia's earlier life, now presented itself in a new allure. No tent nor knapsack, no sleeping bag nor pine-bough bed, no campfire biscuit and boiled water, no treeside evacuations, no hard life on dunes or tundra frost or moldering, wet jungle floor, and no worry of human ambush, animal charge, or insect bite, no worry whatsoever was due him and his on this magnificent, meta-luxury tour of Europe, commencing with Italy. Tintin once knew a famous opera singer from Milano whose stolen jewels he had helped recover, but he himself in all his travels had never been to Italy.

Clavdia had spent time there in her youth, in her wandering years, and had learned to speak Italian as did the Florentines. "*Bocca toscana,*" she had, pronouncing *c*'s as though *h*'s, very elegant her Italian, she had been told, and for that reason she spoke it all the better. "Just to see that face and hear that voice are enough to make me die happy," more than one of her Italian suitors had said to her; it was all too much for them, her beauty and her Italian, spoken as they spoke it but issuing uncannily from the lips of a *forestiera* to give it a perverse charm. They loved her, would die for her or because of her. Her voice, her face, her hair in a splay of fiery flames— her hair was red then—a wild explosion, it drove them mad, the Italian men. She could choose from among them, as she had always chosen, with the willful abandon and recklessness of a woman universally adored.

For a while she chose the Conte di Monte Beni, a young man from an ancient family, his eyes sloe, his hair raven, his passion for her absolute. One day he brought her to his family's ancestral home, a hilltop ruin with an enclosed ruined garden, lizards and rippling thin snakes its tenants. After an afternoon of lovemaking in the bed where he had been born and had spent many languid days of his adolescence, he brought her into the garden and plucked a fig from its tree. With a penknife he made a deep slit that he slowly spread apart with his thumbs. "You open like this ripe fig," the young count said to her, "and your fig is always ripe and always crimson, my red-haired, my redness."

Italian men, expansive, monomaniac, and burning, they were beautiful and gone like the flight and quick red plunge from tree to hedge of a flaming red bird. She had flown beside them in hectic moments of flight but left them when they landed. Her motto: Leave before left. And at all costs, leave. She left the count, too, ardent though he was, in her thrall, as he claimed. She learned that he later withdrew from the world, living alone in his house of decaying rooms and garden, and was cared for by an old family servant who had raised him. What did he do in his house all alone? Clavdia had wondered. The count did not read—not that he disdained books, but his education had never promoted that skill—and he did not race cars or boats, nor did he cook or garden or play at any sports or games. She visited him unexpectedly, as a youth would do, without written announcement or notice, but as he had no telephone, she felt no obligation to be embarrassed should he receive her badly. And should he be rude or surly, she would climb back into her car and speed away over the Tuscan hills to any one of the places where she was surely welcome, where she was longed for.

When he came to the door, finally, his hair slicked back, his lips curled downward, his eyes vacant with the vacancy of the hopeless, Clavdia realized that love was his game, his only sport, indeed his only occupation. She understood, too, that he was enamored with winning this game and that she had been his spoiler. His expression at the door said all that. She need not divine it, it was fully there, his misery at her having left him and his sadness at realizing that while she had come, she had not come to be his lover. He was polite and doleful, and she wanted, she remembered, to laugh. Not from cruelty, this desire to laugh, because she was not cruel to those who loved her, even when she no longer loved them, but from the exaggeration of the man, exaggerated in love and exaggerated in suffering.

There was no tour of the garden this time and no demonstration of analogies of figs or of any other fruit. They sat in his decrepit salon under a Rubens scene of fauns and maidens romping in a glade, in the foreground the figure of an old satyr with flowing white beard dangling a bouquet of grapes over the body of a supine young woman whose smile combined weariness and delight. The family Tiepolos and Titians hung in the obscurity of the heavily cloaked windows and lent nothing of color to the musty gloom of the surroundings.

Yes, he lived here, with Umberto, who fed him *pasta-*

*sciutta* and Dover sole (poached and topped with a caper sauce) brought in from England every other week, and apart from that he saw no one and wished to see even fewer no ones, the count replied to Clavdia's question of how he was spending his days.

He sat facing her in the gloom of the afternoon still in his robe and slippers, speaking little, biting his lip, smoking, distracted, until at last Clavdia announced that she was leaving, since her visit seemed to have found him out of sorts and inconvenienced. She rose to leave, her cigarette still dead in her mouth—he had lit his own without noticing to light hers—and turned to the door where the faint window light caught and seemed to hold her.

But it was his voice, not the light that held her there; she had heard him without realizing that he had spoken, since what he had spoken had penetrated to levels far beneath her consciousness.

"Yes, I'm dying for you. For want of you. Umberto saw you arriving and refused to open the door, so much he hates you for what he thinks you have made of me. Yes, he knows I'm dying for you. For lack of you. You who exist no longer except in my dreams and in my every thought."

When his words filtered themselves up to her consciousness and when she understood not only their meaning but their meaning to the speaker, she unfroze and left him, her heels clicking and clacking on the ancient marble floor, leaving him rapt in his misery. She started for Perugia, then turned about and made for Porto Santo Stefano, then detoured again to race to Rome, her MG buzzing through traffic like an angry red bee. Some of the male drivers tried to pursue and catch up to her, honking their horns, gesticulating and calling out, "*Bambola, stella,* come ride with me." One sped up close to her, shouting, "Slow down, beauty, so I can get a good look at you."

She signaled she was slowing down, smiling at him, but with rage in her heart. After pulling off the road, she waited for him, opening the top buttons of her blouse as his car turned and rolled beside hers so that they were face-to-face.

"Well," she said, "do you want to go? I'm incredibly hot. *Non ho ancora scopato oggi.*"

He could not hide his shock at her boldness and imagined a motive other than love for him. "Ah," he said, "do you want money?"

"Not money," she answered, reaching out to him through the window and pulling him by his tie. "You, I want, with your god's face and body, right now, here in the car."

"You must be crazy, lady. I don't know what you're thinking," he said, revving up his motor and accelerating the car.

"I'm thinking that you are a bigmouth coward and a mama's clown, is what I'm thinking."

He disappeared, and as if he had sent off a warning signal to the others on the road, no other car or person bothered her for the remainder of the journey.

She arrived in Rome after ten to a quiet city and ate some cold pasta with garlic in her apartment. Below her window a mellow light from a restaurant shone on the statue of Giordano Bruno, martyr and Renaissance man of reason. It was reason she wanted, but she was feeling the crazy pull of a madman in love, one who would die for her, was dying for her, his life drying and decoloring like an old, dusty lizard handbag in a hot, sun-filled window of a used-clothes shop on the Tiber.

She climbed into bed with the image of him, of his loneliness and suffering, of his Dover soles wet on the plate before him, wet from his tears and the green caper sauce. She had left him because she feared the sadness his words had made her feel as she had stood there in the doorway trapped in the gloom of his words. That she should suffer this, she who wanted lightness and charm, not misery and darkness, the twin brutes of unrequited love. In what way, she wondered, was she responsible for his misery? Had she misled him or encouraged affection beyond the usual required of impermanent lovers? No. From every perspective she was faultless, her blame only that her being engendered in others wayward emotions she could not regulate. Still, blameless though she was, she felt the count's love for her mattered; no one ever had felt quite as acutely for her as he did, his grief a noble flower in a garden of stones and snakes. With these thoughts she tried to sleep. She slept.

In the morning she knew what to do. Her body knowing it before her mind. She would return to the count and soothe him; if she could not love him, she could help him mend and draw him back to life. She drove the same roads of the previous night and rode them even faster in her rush to appear to him and to make him the present of herself. Car speeds through traffic over hills and bridges, swooshing past inns and motor camps, the hot August sun burning the land and road and tires, igniting, by the power of its incendiary rays, little brush fires along the roadsides, flames leaping and licking her tires as she sings, deep-throated and husky, the "Stabat Mater," singing until she and the song and the ride end at the count's oaken door.

After several loud and declarative knocks, Umberto appears, opening the door the width of a child's hand. The count is indisposed. "Is the count ill?" Clavdia asks apprehensively. No, not ill, indisposed.

Then she will wait for his disposal, Clavdia says.

Yes, the signorina may wait, wait wherever she wishes but not inside. She shall wait elsewhere, she says in cool fury, but she will return in a hour or so, and when she does, she is sure the count will be available, or Umberto and the count may start to look about for replacements for their heads. She withdraws and drives to the town to look in the shop windows and have lunch and maybe buy a pair of soft gloves. Hot hot hot and dusty, and it's August, nearly everything is closed for *ferragosto,* restaurants, shops, even the bakery. Then she remembers the open-air terrace of the little hotel where sometimes she and the count had spent afternoons in the cheapest room in the house—he being too frugal for a more expensive bed and she unable to pay for one because it was against the count's principles to have a woman pay for anything while in his company—and she goes there, leaving her car to cool under the shade of a medlar tree. Crowded tables in the patio, and there, at one of them, under the shade of umbrella, is the count, lifting a forkful of *caprese* to his mouth.

And with him, sipping a glass of amber-colored wine glowing as if distilled from sunshine, a woman made from sunshine and red gold. She was youth itself, sweet as the muscatel wine she was drinking, wine made from the grapes of the count's ancient vineyard, several bottles of which rested in the hotel's cellar for the count's exclusive use. Clavdia had sipped this rare wine at the very table and chair where the youth was presently growing even more radiant from its powers. The count was now speaking to the young woman, half singing his words, one hand caressing her golden hair, the other tracing the contours of her face. Clavdia read his lips, read a text she had heard before when addressed to her, lines of endearment, sentences of love, phrases of longing.

"I'm pleased at your recovery," Clavdia said, speaking in English.

"Ah! It is you, my dear Clavdia," he answered, also in
English, seeming unsurprised to see her. "No, I am not much
recovered, and I would be home reposing but for a visit from
my niece here, who deserves a more charming atmosphere
than the confines of my gloomy quarters."

The young woman understood nothing of what they had
said and remained smiling pleasantly throughout the exchange. Clavdia addressed her in Italian, noting how fortunate the young lady was to have so doting an uncle, especially
at a time when her uncle, the count, had recently suffered
such bereavements and griefs and had been all but interred
in his castle because of them. What a soothing nurse she must
be. The young woman's smile vanished and seemed to reap-
pear, in exaggerated form, on the count, who was busying
himself keeping the young woman from leaving the table.

"Good-bye, Count, and best wishes to you, young lady,"
Clavdia said.

She was leaving, too, the young woman said. In fact,
would Clavdia mind if she joined her? And join Clavdia she
did, all the way to Rome, where, in fact, she lived and where
she had met the count in some dusty sculpture gallery. Hilda,
for that was the young woman's name, and Clavdia became
friends, sisters famous for beauty. The red and the gold, as
they were known, broke hearts that fall and splintered several
more until the following spring, when Clavdia took up with
Hilda's brother, a golden youth more in love with Clavdia
than the count had ever been, and called a truce to love and
its battles. That was Clavdia's Italy.

Now she would return there with Tintin and explore with
him its ruins and the terrain of her memories. She would
return to where youth and beauty held sway in all matters,
for nowhere in the world did people love beauty as much as

did the Italians, but now it would not be her beauty that won the day but the power of her money.

Money ushered them to the best hotels. Tintin marveled at Venice from his terrace breakfast at the Gritti Palace and spent the afternoon shopping for gloves with Clavdia. In the evening they hired a gondola and glided along the canals and palaces. Tintin held Clavdia in his arms and looked up at the stars, where a strange and new constellation formed before his eyes. There, in the purple-black sky, was Snowy, with bone in jaw, climbing the higher reaches of heaven. Now he was there, fixed forever in human sight, with Bear and Lion and Dipper.

The gondolier glanced to where Tintin was pointing out the dog's outlines to Clavdia and exclaimed in a voice loud and familiar: *"Uffa, anche qua, non mi lascia mai in pace questa bestia."*

Now not even the romantic scarf—worn against the malignant night vapors of the canal, as he had explained to his passengers on their boarding—masking half the gondolier's face could disguise any longer Settembroglio-Settembrini. Tintin and Clavdia rose to him in that moment of recognition, but he had already steered the vessel to the quay, deftly alighted, and disappeared into the Venetian night.

"What a night of miracles," exclaimed Tintin. "Snowy and Settembrini, what will fate think of next!"

They left Venice in the mood of wonders, feeling themselves in a state of grace. Attentive to her as he always was, Tintin grew yet more solicitous of Clavdia as she seemed to tire easily and forget or misplace her eyeglasses, her hearing aid, her toothbrush. When they reached Rome, she recalled she had left her passport in Florence, but on phoning there, she discovered she had left her jewelry behind in the hotel safe and that her passport was in fact sewn into the lining of her Hermès jacket, a precautionary trick employed when she was young and traveling alone through wild cities.

Now she and Tintin walked through the Campo dei Fiori, where she had lived at nineteen or eighteen, *tutta sola,* all alone and happy in that quarter of flower stalls and fruits. And there above them now was the very apartment, the balcony lined with flowers in terra-cotta pots, the French windows gleaming. She had left her youth imprinted there on terrace and marble floor and apartment walls. Perhaps, she mused, she could scratch some flakes of her sojourn from the walls and retrieve from them the molecules of her youth.

They lunched, then continued the tour of personal and historical sites, stopping many times to rest. Against Clavdia's objections, Tintin finally called the hotel for a car, which drew up smartly before the café where they were again stopping to rest. Clavdia wanted to see the Catacombs of St. Calixtus before calling it a day. She had been there once, and it had left a deep impression on her—or a man she had met there had left an impression on her, Tintin did not quite understand which—and so they went, down into the caves where in coves and niches the remains of monks had been stacked like dried codfish. A sarcophagus held a desiccated monk still in his moldy habit, his teeth intact under a horrid grin.

Resting on his chest, a placard, on which he had written, some two hundred years before, the legend: "As you are, so I was. As I am, so shall you be." Rather than sadden or depress him, Tintin found the communication apt and vital. The force of the truism proved tonic. His spirits lifted, as indeed, they had during the whole of the journey. "How noble, and how beautiful death is when cast in the role of

truth teller, more beautiful than that which lives and lies,"
he pronounced.

"Never to see the sky and never to drink the wines of
spring, never to buy gloves, and never to bathe in the afternoon glare of the sun as you and I fall asleep in a sweat of
love, no, Tintin, not noble," Clavdia said in the car on their
way back to the hotel. "Never to see Marlinspike and the
sea where the captain made his last fiery voyage, nor hear
the waves crash on Marlinspike's shore when in the night I
turn to you and see your sweet face and smell your honey
smell," she added in the elevator. "And never to see your
Tintin face," she concluded, gasping in the giant hotel bed,
where her breath and her life forever left her.

Tintin carried her ashes to Marlinspike and scattered them
over the sea and through the forest lanes where they rode,
keeping a portion of her dust in an urn, which he buried
beside Snowy and the headstone of the captain's empty grave.

Little Tintin reappeared with wife and children, and after
some consoling words broached the subject of Marlinspike's
subdivision, citing especially the hugeness of the estate and
the presently reduced number of inhabitants. Tintin was
weary and promised never to consider the matter in his lifetime or at any time thereafter. Litigation it would be then.
A battle in the courts, the last recourse left him, Little Tintin
declared. He and wife turned away and left. Tintin imagined
he heard in their departing footsteps the thunderous booms
of dynamite exploding Marlinspike with its parks and sea
dunes. He watched, as he had years before, his son's car, the
most expensive ever made, speed away down the long drive-
way, and then he went to the upstairs galley and set about
uncrating and hanging the artworks he had collected in his
youth.

He once had thought of paintings as colorful decorations, priceless wall coverings for the many naked walls of Marlinspike. Even after Clavdia had come to live with him and imposed beauty and order there, Marlinspike's walls still remained largely bare, paintings meaning little more to Clavdia than to Tintin. Now he roamed his collection and devoted hours to studying each of the paintings, waking up at times in the early morning to look again at a picture that had flashed through his head even as he slept. A large Matisse canvas drew him back many times. There figures nude and free danced on a field of blue, women and men their arms held above them, hands joined in a whirling slow dance through the sluggish air of time. Of youth and life it made him think, naturally; of the dance of life, too, and the way that the dance slows and speeds; of joy and its sad twin it made him think; and finally, and at the heart, of Clavdia, death, and beauty it made him think.

The soul of beauty takes many forms, he thought, as the tower was rising. Stone by stone it rose at the tipmost edge of the highest cliff overlooking the ocean. He went to it every day to watch the masons and carpenters turn the stones into his other, circular home, his tight room fronting the sea with a glass so thin as to seem invisible. There he slept and woke, with no earth beneath him, suspended in the fullness of sea and sky, the weld joining each a narrow scar his eyes did not distinguish.

That afternoon the sky went gray, and great sheets of rain made a waterfall of his window; red lightning cracked through the great broil of sea sky, and thunder boomed through the vast park. The tower shook and slightly swayed in the rushing winds. Tintin first feared that stone and glass would tumble into the mad sea below, but then he thought he would welcome the plunge and let the elements take him where they would. He'd ride sovereign over them on a matchstick or they'd break him and whirl him into a jelly of bones and dreams. Toward midnight the storm abated, and the night turned into a crystal dome.

Tintin searched the sky for Snowy and found him there, but the bone in the dog's mouth had disappeared, a glove dangled in its place, and farther along in the direction of Snowy's climb, or, indeed, what Snowy was mounting toward, stretched the hand of the inclining and waiting Clavdia.

# Chapter XI

In the chill night before dawn they briefly woke. Not fully, not with the clarity of waking that brings the new day sharply to life and leaves the dream of sleep forgotten in the haze of the past. They woke with the recognition of what they had dreamed, each feeling they had lived the dream as fully as if they had experienced it in waking life. They *had* experienced it, and it was now etched forever in their living tissue, though perhaps not forever in their living memory.

For a moment they looked at each other in the full wonder of what they had just dreamed—had lived—and with the drowsy indulgence of those who would wake and continue living, they returned to sleep, the memory of their dream fading with each breath.

# Chapter XII

That morning, when he finally woke, Tintin found himself—
how he did not remember—returned to his own room, to
his own bed. For his bed mate, he had not Clavdia but Snowy,
who, chilled in the dark chill of early morning, had crept
under the covers of his master's then empty bed. It was to
Snowy's woolly ear that Tintin's sighs and vows of love had
been made in the razor light of dawn, not to the woman who
had ushered him, still in the drowse of sleep dream and love,
to his own quarters.

Haddock's banging at the door brought Tintin away from
his sleep sharply. It was breakfast time again. Too soon for
Tintin, as was anything so ordinary after an evening of miracles. But to breakfast he went and to the very table and with
the very companions of the previous day. (A day? A whole
life had passed and another had begun in the span of those
several hours!) Silence and torpor ruled, the meal consumed
at a sluggish pace. Tintin lifted his eyes several times from
his plate to direct them at the woman who sat erectly and
distractedly opposite him, her hand grazing from time to time
the sturdy hand of Herr Peeperkorn.

Silent, languid, dull, the morning meal, yet for Tintin it bespoke activity. When he first saw Clavdia at the table, he was on the open sea, sails straining in the full, heady wind. She soon joined him at the wheel, the two riding the plunging waves, their swift schooner shivering beneath them as she ran the storm. Still later, while the others dawdled over coffee, Tintin was in his prison cell, alone, in his usual solitary confinement, where he had been born and where he was destined to die. Suddenly the cell door sprang open, and now he was waving his farewells to those envious inmates left behind in their iron cages, now he was descending the metal stair leading directly to the warden's office, where a huge, bearded man rose from behind his fatherly desk to greet him and warmly send him off into the world ready for the enterprise of happiness.

Before yet further adventures ensued, the meal was pronounced over, done, finished, quite. Everyone agreed, Tintin as well, that a stroll was in order, an excursion at once touristical and tonic over the hills and declivities of the Inca ruins.

Single file and slowly they climbed, Naptha in the lead, followed by Settembrini, Clavdia between Peeperkorn and Tintin, holding the hand of each, Haddock and Snowy trailing behind, until they reached the pinnacle of Huayna Picchu, the ancient lookout post of the Inca city. Snowy skirted the edge of the precipice, anxiously peering down the vast space to the jungle and river below. He whined and breathed shortly.

"Snowy, what's the matter, old boy? Why this fit?" Tintin asked, breaking the morning silence.

"As do all animals," Naptha answered, "your dog senses blood. From this very cliff Inca justice hurled Inca criminals two thousand feet to the floor below."

"Death rituals interest me," Peeperkorn declared somberly, his expression pinched. "I have seen many kinds of deaths in my time, quite. Your ordinary deathbed variety— a little crackle and wheeze, the raspy expiration, very commonplace that signaling off into eternity, and very orderly is that death, a little whisk of the broom and the matter's clean and gone, whereas your suicide's usually a messy affair. Very few go out with grace; most leave their carcasses behind for someone else to clean up, like the weekend guest who's befouled his room and leaves you, smiling, suitcase in hand, to discover later the debris of his stay."

"Blinding planks, briny pegs—'nother squall approaches," Haddock interjected, his eyes skyward, as if reading the clouds.

"It's a perfectly clear day, Captain. What are you saying?" Tintin asked.

"That's his little joke on me," Peeperkorn said goodnaturedly. "Have I been meandering again, my good captain? You are quite right to drop anchor on my drifting discourse."

"No offense, Mr. Peeperkorn. Just that when you fellows set to tacking morbid channels, I feel the wind leave me sails. Becalmed I am in a cold sea of sleepy weeds and sloshy brine, and I go whistling at me boots."

"To the Incas," continued Naptha, pretending to disregard the interruptions, "a criminal was beyond the pale of understood humanity, a creature merely retaining the form of the man known before venturing into the illegal act, a contagion to be exorcised. And to this end there is no telling the passion of the community prior to the execution—the laments and shrieks of the man's family, the wailing of his former friends. The mountains clamored with howling dogs and bawling children. Timbrels, drums of stretched tiger skin, silver flutes, jade whistles marched in procession along a course lined with priests, nobles, artisans, while the criminal sang his death chant, the song of his expiation and his hope: 'Receive me, earth, receive me, sky, to one and all I say goodbye.'

"And then to the cliff, the binding of the arms and legs, the fateful shove and final fall. At once all return to their accustomed lives—the twisted faces of the mourners now placid, the howling children now still, the world again as before, ordered, reasonable. None claim the corpse; none bury or burn it or drape it in trees. Far away from the city, it remains to rot and to be eaten and picked away, so far below that no reminding stench wafts to the sweet living mountains where men and women till the hillsides and tend children and fires."

"I tell you, gentlemen and lady," Settembrini said heatedly, "that this is sheer fantasy! Another of Herr Naptha's insane fabrications. Amazing how he distorts, to suit his rabid reactionary head, the facts concerning a culture he knows full well was a model of tyranny, repression, whose aim was the subjugation, not the elevation, of the human spirit."

"And I assure you all," Naptha answered, "that where there is order the spirit rises. Order, however, produces no pendulum swings from despair to joy but instills in the individual and in the community soul a mood of constant well-being, which, after all, is an elevation from the normal condition of those living in disorderly societies, the mood, that is, of daily uneasiness and unwellness. The democracies breed such morbid feelings, leaving the individual to believe himself free when this freedom is merely his right to confusion and misery."

"Oh, my!" exclaimed Settembrini, holding his head in his hands. "Oh, yes, the goodness is in you but so bound with meanness and anger. To hear you say those words fills me with hope, for you must admit, finally, that democracy may breed reform where it once lay broken. May your goodwill ever reign, Herr Naptha."

"In our time," continued Naptha, disregarding the Italian's benediction, "we have seen the wise application of the laws of human nature employed in a much-maligned state, one that gave broad room to the dynamism of those who, by dint of intelligence and will, would make their way to high economic and social planes, a state that rewarded a person's love of family and homeland, a state that defined human dignity as that balance between individualist license and responsibility to the community.

"You, Settembrini, condemn Fascist Italy and dismiss its achievements, the very achievements that had they been made under the aegis of state capitalism or democratic socialism, you would be savoring and pronouncing their virtues. Instead you call Il Duce a murderous buffoon and denigrate the social reforms he engineered as mere sops to keep the bourgeois in power."

"The clown who killed," Settembrini sputtered, "that jaw-jutting, strutting ham in uniform, that is the man you extol! No, this is too much."

"Il Duce's vainglorious posturings do not affect me—each to his own mode of theatricality, I say, for no man is exempt from some form of histrionics—but his actions do address me. I speak, of course, of Mussolini's actions prior to his entering the shameful African and European theaters of war. For in what dictatorship of our times do you find a regime as benign toward its people and its enemies alike? So long divided between upper and lower boot, Italy knew no leader concerned with the joining of the two, with the mending of the lower, especially, which through the years had been made to wear down so that the upper could better shine like a gentleman's leathered calf. Il Duce set out to repair the worn-out sole so that the entire boot might stride among the nations of the world in dignity. Need I remind you that only under that man's rule did Italy not feel itself the *pensione* of the industrial world, the inn for every foreigner who came to pluck the ripest figs and to drain off the Tuscan sun."

"A deceiver, a liar, a confidence man, a bully, a despot, a murderer, there's your protector of his people—my people," Settembrini cried.

"Nonsense! As for tyranny, injustice, class genocide, who is it that killed millions in the name of social and economic democracy only to create a new inequality? Was it the square-jawed Italian or the Georgian who killed off peasant and worker and intellectual alike, who murdered his enemies from vanity? The Italian only prescribed castor oil and beatings, and death for a few really bad ones, the terrorists. Every regime must protect itself against subversion, and the fascist is no less deserving of such self-protection."

Settembrini straightened himself and brushed the sleeve of his sorry coat. His voice trembled as he spoke. "Class interests, state interests. Murderous abstractions. What of human interests, my own living self-interest? I wish neither the individual nor the state to oppress me."

"Well, my friends," Peeperkorn said gently, "let's cease all Old World noise and share together the splendors of this vista, this grand sky and vast, plunging abyss."

The group, after some huffing by the two antagonists, gathered obediently at the cliff's edge. Tintin felt a brushing of his hand and turned to see Clavdia smiling at him.

"Beauty is incomparable, crime, criminals, or no. Beauty needs no historical gloss, sublime, divine, out of time. Isn't that so, young sleuth?"

"Quite so, Herr Peeperkorn," Tintin answered. But, then, he heard himself say, his voice distant, recognizable yet unfamiliar, "What is the beauty of nature compared with that of the beauty of woman? The beauty of woman, which leaves me, leaves me—"

"Speechless!" interjected Settembrini.

"A blabbering fool," Naptha chimed in.

"Leaves me—"

"Helpless," ventured Peeperkorn.

"No, no, leaves me."

"Ah," said Clavdia, "this beauty departs from you, yes?"

"It was there, in me," Tintin said, "and was flowing through my tissues, the beauty of oceans at dusk, of triangles. Then it left me, and joined us here," he continued, blushing, his eyes averted from Clavdia's, his voice returning to itself.

"Is it this talk of crime that leads you to the theme of the beauty of woman?" Naptha asked mischievously.

"Oh! Crime and women, I know little firsthand of that particular relationship," Tintin answered.

"Crimes of passion not your sort of stew, eh! Well, what would you say is your actual line of expertise?" Peeperkorn asked. "Who are your protagonists? Criminals of the street, pickpockets, muggers, cutthroats, bicycle thieves, and the like?"

"He wouldn't dirty his hands with such minor filth," exclaimed Clavdia. "Why would you suppose such a thing? This is Tintin you are speaking to. Tintin, and not some detective you hire to smell people's bed sheets."

"No offense, none intended, none. It's the anemic air up here. . . . What could I have been thinking!"

"No injury, sir. But to answer you, in my line, my métier, I encounter—seek out—criminals less of the manual and more of the cerebral kind. Wrongdoers on the brainy scale, who abhor and shun deeds of personal violence. I've noticed that each commits the crime to which he has access. Thus the poor, whose life is in the streets, engage in crimes of the streets, those sometime violent assaults and holdups, as well as those more pacific muggings and pickpocketings. To the clerks and persons working in offices go the larding of petty-cash vouchers, the pilferings of stationery, paper clips, and staples; to the middle management, the inflating of expense accounts, the cooking of books, and outright embezzlement . . . well, you understand my drift.

"My types," continued Tintin, "seize governments of nations by bribe and corruption or by engineering revolutions. They are not criminals common to our streets. They do not walk beside us in the thoroughfares of the day or brush by us in the glittering commotion of the urban night. We never see their photographs in newspapers or magazines; no press heralds their marriages and deaths; no advertisements announce their dealings, legitimate or otherwise. It is sheer pedantry of me to study them since they are an obscurantist breed. Very recondite fellows, hermetic, one may say with justice. Scholars, they are, whose subject is the nefarious circuitry of power and sophisticated misrule, for they love dominion perversely. Shy, like true scholars, they prefer the studious and clandestine accommodations of secluded châteaux in Brittany or Normandy or some or another English shire to the ostentatious bureaus found so widely in cities given to international finance and interlocking, corporate consortium. Their minions are legion, and it is their upper-level minions, not they, who occupy, in various guises and facades, the grand offices in the major capitals of the world representing the legitimate-seeming enterprises of their otherwise illegal, filthy doings. Then, to abbreviate somewhat, there is an order of underling, the subspecies of international criminality, the lumpen criminal, if you will, the eyes and tentacles of the vast empire, who perform (never knowing the purpose or motive behind their commissioned acts) the requisite blindings, bone breakings, teeth shatterings, kidnappings, and killings. The Captain and I have crossed paths with many of this class—often one must cut through them in order to advance to the superior levels—but felons of this low rung generally do not wander the streets in search of random victims. And thus criminals of the street are a genre apart from my specialization."

"And grateful I am for these nice distinctions, and glad you have made them for us," Naptha said. "And all the better to introduce and clarify my prospectus. You have omitted in your discourse that criminal species that count as profit not merely goods and money but the thrill of violence, the passion of cruelty, those who are as soon content to kill for a shoestring as for a gold bar.

"But leaving this aside, let me speak of the bizarre way the liberal democracies have in treating their thieves, their assaulters—the lowest on the rung of malefactors. Claiming that poverty drives criminals of this order to steal and murder, these democracies attempt to deal compassionately with these criminals, yet this kindness only encourages the criminals further since because their actions go largely unpunished, they undertake greater crimes without fear of punishment. Bolder and bolder these criminals become until eventually they need no weapons to pose their crimes, needing only to present their demands to the cowering victim. Why not resist? you ask. Can the aged resist? Can the ordinary person resist, faced with the loss of an eye, of teeth, of life itself?

"And suppose," Naptha continued, his cheeks glowing, "one does resist and even turns the tables and apprehends the criminal and gives him to the law. In these democracies there is no guarantee that the criminal will ever be incarcerated! Yes, this is true, though I see from your smiles and smirks your incredulity. And if he is incarcerated, the sentences are so brief and the criminal so angry, more maddened, vice-filled, and fearless than when he entered his cell, that there is danger of his returning to revenge himself on the victim, stabbing or shooting him and his family in their very house. The liberal democracies neither adequately suppress their criminals nor attempt to destroy the roots of crime, poverty, and social misery. Liberal societies reason themselves out of their instinct for self-preservation, commit suicide, swallow their own human poison."

"And what is your antidote?" Settembrini asked. "For I'm sure you have one."

"Terror. Terrorize the malefactors as they do us. Not revenge but simple, impersonal, painless evacuation of the poison in the body social. Restore the penal colonies and the labor camps; restore corporal punishment. Let the wrongdoer feel the gnawing humiliation of a public flogging; let him know that if he raises his hand against the community, he shall receive a full dozen or two that his back shall never forget—and start the beatings at school age, when they leave maximum impression of pain and shame. Restore shame to the culture. And for all those who repeatedly attack society and for whom all efforts at correction have failed, kill—let's not mince words—kill them as quickly as and soon after the commission of their crime as possible."

"Yes, kill, kill everyone," Settembrini said, his voice trembling and soft. "That is all your brutal kind understands, to kill. The voice that reasons and soothes alone can heal the angry world. How few who say, 'Yes, rob me of my goods, but never let my anger seek to revenge the loss in kind greater than the theft, for trinkets may be replaced but lives never.' "

"Do you think it's trinkets they're after? Colored glass and hand mirrors, necklaces of paste? A soothing word, a kind gesture for the canaille, the brutes who rape and murder anyone weaker than they? They, my friend, wish to do mayhem simply because they were born. Because, my friend, the short hate the tall, the ugly the handsome, the poor the rich, all that is low loathes the higher, and most of all, the low hates itself, and with a rage that, were it harnessed, could level mountains and cities to pebbles and dust."

"Well, you both," said Peeperkorn cheerfully, bowing to the now-silent antagonists, "seem to know so much of these matters. Why, a regular compendium of philosophies you are. Most rewarding, I assure you, to stand here by this historical precipice and receive, free of charge, I may add, such informative views. This young man, this very one standing beside me, guileless, earnest, and dreamy, he must share my appreciation for what learning you have broadcast here among us. N'est-ce pas, young detective? Quite an education on human nature and other such related matters."

"I would have supposed, Tintin, that the investigation of the criminal mind and all matters pertaining to criminality would be your major and absorbing preoccupation," interjected Naptha. "And I regret you did not complete your earlier discourse on these matters, for they interest me not a little, touching as they do on issues whose source is the study of sin, salvation, and the soul."

"How marvelously you put it!" exclaimed Tintin. "I've never really thought my subject extended to the depths you suggest, though in the annals of the literature of crime there is, I'm reminded, a proponent of such an approach, good Father Brown. He who could see in a person's face or gait, in the way a man tied his shoelaces, the workings of conscience, the measure of his guilt and his innocence. Father Brown's method is the intuitive, his purpose, the salvational. Yes, I long ago studied his cases and approaches but found them inapplicable to my own detecting endeavors."

"Bravo, in a newfound voice you express the essential format of the fascistic Chesterton," declared Settembrini, "locating in the so-called intuitive antiempirical methodology of his hero the antirational rationale that so inspires the prophets of instinct and blood knowing, this good Father Brown, as you called him, being no less than the priest of darkness."

"I must confess these are claims that have eluded me, for I thought Father Brown a sweet man and good-natured, but I've been troubled by the inapplicability of his approach in matters where a network of criminals operating in areas outside one's ken is involved, for surely one cannot study faces and personalities that are not directly before you, seated beside you on a park bench, let us say. Thus in cases of large interlocking international criminal organizations whose chiefs are located in several nations and whose agents number in the hundreds, Father Brown's method is inapplicable. And then, too, I am not concerned with punishment or with the spiritual fate of the transgressor, only with the criminal's severance and elimination from the criminal operation."

"Yes," Naptha said, "but that apart, I'm sure we all would like to know what interests you in this line of work. What, may I ask, is your motivation in tracking and apprehending criminals?"

"A propensity for action which would otherwise enlist itself in such activities as yachting, chess playing, stamp, coin, postcard collecting, bird watching—that is, I might have become an alcoholic, a psychoanalytic patient, a rose gardener, a polo player, a Sunday painter—"

"Enough, you've established your point quite sufficiently," said Naptha.

"Not finished yet," said Tintin, facing down his interrupter, "for to answer fully, I must explain how in my early youth I thought the world a happy place, where apart from grief beyond one's control—the death and loss of those one loved, the fall from fortune or from health, blindness, or the loss of limbs—all human sadness caused by humans was remediable. Thus to extirpate the wrongdoer from the community of the good was to restore the community to health. How and why wrongdoers came into being, whether by nature or circumstance, was a matter indifferent to me, for the excitement of their pursuit and the knowledge that their elimination from the world restored—even in small part—peace to the world gave me satisfaction.

"How little I understood the workings of the community I had wished to serve, how less I knew of the human heart, the least known of all, my own. And now, in retrospect, I think my chiefmost aim, and the noble cloak it had provided me, were no more than a concealment for my restlessness, for what would I have done with my stunted, skimpy life had I not had this purpose and this self-appointed commission but amuse myself with the pastimes of my leisured solitude? And now, through some strange transforming thing that has happened and is happening to me, these illuminating conversations with you, perhaps, which have served me such abundant nourishing stuff, or because of these mountains, whose casual air may have set off some chemical spark that, yeastlike, makes rise this arrested flesh, or perhaps through some other unknown influence, I begin to form new thoughts and new purposes, as yet inchoate but promising to cohere and to bring me to new vision.

"I have come to learn through observing you and listening to your conversations (and from a dream I think I had) that discord, violence, and passion rule in even those innocent of wishing to do wrong. How strange I did not understand that this discord wreaks more savage havoc than any mere theft or assault, for while the individual criminal is, by comparison, easily locatable and plucked from the community he or she infects, the community itself is rife with readiness to do mayhem in the name of right-headedness and principle. How, then, may remedy be applied to the community at large, this civilized world, I mean?

"Perhaps I should puff a stout English pipe, blow pensive rings at hearth's fender, and swirl my brandy till idle, indolent slumber takes me. Keep myself at home, I mean, among my books and my toys, with the tight captain and the dog, innocent and loving both, companions of my ignorant youth and comrades of my premature dotage, for dotage it is to live without desire or without wishing to inform each hour with personal intent.

"What wrong and what wrongdoer," Tintin continued sadly, "are there left to stalk when now I know I would need to stalk the tracks of every living human, for all are guilty, even as they sleep, guilty of mischief done or yet to be done? The human womb breeds human monsters, sucking eel mouths of desire and willfulness. Why, it disgusts me now to eat meat. I am a criminal of the table and the plate, the eater of animal legs and breasts and flanks, but yet worse than even I live in cozy respectability, and worse than many murderers I have known live to receive honors and banquets for deeds that the world deems licit but which obdurate criminals, whether from lack of ingenuity or means of sufficient badness, would shun.

"Whom, then, should I now pursue? Let the people know their jaguar prince, in whatever guise he comes, has come. Let the forest oak, the jungle mahogany, the tender sapling cleave the ax that strikes it; let the whale and the seal, the otter, and the fox render mad with wails the hunter; let the insolent and the deceivers, the wasters and the spoilers, the greedy and the ignorant go and beg their food from those they've injured; let them live long and racked in memories of their white plates heaped with tasty dishes.

"Punishment shall know no class exception, shall excuse no man or woman for reason of high birth, or for his lack of education and good breeding, but his deed shall condemn him.

"Among the crimes I consider worthy of severe punishment are: the beating of animals; the misuse of children; the injuring of the old; the extirpation of trees; the mutilation or otherwise defacing of hills, mountains, natural rock formations; the dumping of streams, rivers, lakes, and oceans with chemical and industrial wastes; the general befouling and rending of our atmosphere. For such offenses I warrant the penalty, for first offenders, of hard labor with long sentences, labor that restores, in some measure, what has been robbed from the community, its fresh water, its pure air. Vandals and desecrators of public monuments, parks, cemeteries, vehicles of transportation, I commit to hard labor until said destructions have been financially and physically recompensed to the community; let vandals sweep and wash the streets, the metro, all places of thoroughfare and concourse, let them repair, repave, mend roads, fill potholes and other such crevices, yes, and let them weed out rank gardens and rake the autumn leaves. Punishment, too, for the creators and purveyors of defective and faulty products, punishment for shoddy workmanship and for the malingerer and the shiftless, for the idle parasites, the time server, for all those who share neither in the formation of goods nor in the production of industry but gain from the chancy flow of profit and loss—the speculator, the middlemen who do all sorts of middling services. And all those who destroy nature shall be the last of their destructive breed. The lion and dolphin, the elephant and whale shall replace them.

"I enjoin you to think on these matters, as shall I, for there is much yet for me to learn before the jaguar leaves its secret and provincial lair and takes for its path the open world. How paltry have been my aims, how narrow my scope, how mistaken to loop only the sick branch when the malignant offense must be ripped from its thick, sappy roots.

"You appear shocked by my words, by my thoughts, my companions, excepting perhaps, you, Madame Clavdia, who sit here as if disjoined from the rest; your mind, if I read it properly, a screen of blankness and repose. I bid you, let us stay and discourse among ourselves whether criminals are born or made and how villains find their way in the dark, why sparrows converse with the dead and whether Satan still dreams of winning heaven."

"Stay all, but do excuse me," Clavdia said. "The thinness of the air and the prospect of this high view produce the most dizzying effects. I shall, nonetheless, make my way back to the hotel alone quite happily and safely."

"Leaping lariats! I'll tow you to port, madame, if you'll navigate the course. Me compass's spinning in this lofty altitude." Removing his cap, the captain bowed.

"Me, too, Madame Clavdia. I'll join you, too, if I may," Tintin added eagerly, his voice high-pitched, his manner the same as if nothing he had said moments before had been said.

"Let us all depart. Let us together pick our way from this botanic growth. You, Linnaeus, and you, Tournefort," said Peeperkorn, pointing majestically to Tintin and Naptha, "shall be in the advance of our procession homeward, for having snared us in the webs of your classifications, who more deserving to blaze the trail to the simple pleasures of our inn?"

"I leave, but under protest," Settembrini said, "and with the claim of future rejoinder to Herr Naptha's calumnies, for to leave evil words and thoughts to spread without contest is to collaborate in their corrosive triumphs."

The group formed rank. With Tintin and Naptha in advance, Haddock and Clavdia behind, Peeperkorn and Settembrini in the rear, they proceeded slowly down the narrow trail. But it was Snowy, with his fits and starts, with sudden bursts of acceleration and just as rapid halts to ferret a salamander from under a rock, who actually led the way.

# Chapter XIII

[Afternoon of the same day.]

The signs were thick. Reason with them as he might, he could not deny their insistent presence. There were almost too many signs, each worthy of attention. Only yesterday a condor, gripping a two-headed snake in its mouth, swept the heights of Machu Picchu three times, and at that moment an Indian from a nearby village gave birth to a daughter who spoke in several languages.

Still, the lieutenant resisted. It was too large a matter, too profound to bear, that destiny had chosen him to witness and aid the coming. How could he be certain that the stories his grandfather had told him were true? How could he be sure that the old man's memory was not blurred or that he had not corrupted the ancient prophecy with inventions of his own, or those of others before him? Weighing most in his doubts, he admitted, was his disbelief that he, baked of common clay, undistinguished by birth and accomplishment, should be the knower and first guide. Yet again, the omens and signs were there, seen by all and fully understood only by him.

Lieutenant dos Amantes thought these things as he sat drinking alone in the patio of his favorite cantina in a village three miles below Machu Picchu. It was market day. He spied Naptha limping through the bustling stalls. A young woman with a child at her breast squatted in the shade of a stone wall. As Naptha passed, she stretched out her arm and opened her hand. Naptha scowled and accelerated his limping pace. Presently another familiar figure appeared: Settembrini. In the bright light of day the lieutenant saw clearly that the Italian's pants were soiled and frayed and that his scuffed shoes sloped sharply down at the heels.

Settembrini bowed and glanced furtively at the woman's naked breast. Then, suddenly, he raised his head and swept his eyes over the cloudless sky as he fingered his waistcoat in search of a coin. But either the object of his search was not to be found or Settembrini had undergone a change of heart, for he resumed his walk, eyes skyward.

Lieutenant dos Amantes shifted in his seat and muttered. Snowy suddenly appeared at the lieutenant's foot, and the dog raised himself on his hind legs.

"You're a good one, aren't you?" the lieutenant said respectfully. "Like your master, I think."

Snowy rubbed his snout against the soldier's thigh and gave out a little sharp whine.

"*Hasta luego,*" the lieutenant called out as Snowy suddenly trotted across the street and disappeared among the stalls.

Dos Amantes spoke to his creamy-blue drinking cup as if it were wired to the deepest veins of the world, linking his wavy voice to the trees and brush of the surrounding jungles, to boulders and canyons, to the farthest sandy stretches of his country's foggy coast. In his mind he made this cup the intimate ear of a universe hungry for news.

"Men and women come and go, all quarrels and all mem-

ories of even the most hideous deeds are forgotten, and all
the love of the world is forgotten also, all this I know. How
much more light there is when one soft word is spoken, when
one warm caress is given."

The sun was setting, the market closing down. The lieutenant had lined before him a dozen cups and saucers. And
he had set before them a barricade of shot glasses, now empty.
The young mother sat where she had sat that morning, begging from all those who passed by.

Here was a tableau inspiring of discourse. Here a theme to
pluck on, a furious rhetorical serenade to be strummed late
into the night: There had been no beggars and no beggary
before the Europeans came. Nor wives deserted by their hus-
bands. No hunger, except when the land went mad and
scorched the tilled terraced fields or uprooted the corn with
torrents of brackish rain. But they came, those Spanish, white
and sickly, greedy for stupid, dead gold. Greedy and mean,
and jealous of each other. They were the least of their kind,
the most abject and most vicious—and the most ignorant of
a stupefyingly ignorant people. They knew nothing of the
stars except how to find the great poles by them, they could
not count the flow of days that made a cycle about the sun,
and thus they did not know the fine line of hours between
one season and the next, and thus they planted and harvested
with the precision of spider monkeys. If one of their men
tumbled off his horse and split open his head, they would
leave him to die in the brush, moaning and calling for his
mother or the mother of the strange god they so much resembled, bearded and white and sickly. Of the arts of healing
they knew nothing except to leave to chance what chance
would take. And this they called the will of their God. Of a
finely shaped bowl they cared nothing except to curse it for
being clay and not the metal gold. And finely worked bowls

of gold they melted down and poured into molds and shipped away the insensible ingots. Pillage they knew best, and rape and drunkenness, all things in the negative spirit. How to torture a man until he revealed his little hoard of coins or buckle of gold, how to maim a slave so that he must forever walk on his hands and knees, his useless legs trailing in the dust.

He ordered another coffee. Very strong, like simmering tar itself, to shake him from his sentimentality, from the Spanish infection of lyricism and self-pity. They gave us that, too, the weeping self-pity that brings us to wail about lost love, or the thousand injuries of a kiss not yet won, or the love that endures beyond the grave, love that lives in the bones even after death, even after the bones have become dust. " '*Polvo serán, mas polvo enamorado,*' " he said to the night.

The waiter brought his coffee and asked whether he wanted him to clear the table.

"Never," dos Amantes shouted. "I want these objects here today and tomorrow and until I say to take them—in thirty-eight years perhaps, or maybe never." He ordered another drink, a large pisco sour in a water glass. A thought struck him, and he shouted into the cantina, "A guitar. Bring me a big one."

There was some laughter at the bar, and dos Amantes remembered that no one in the café owned a guitar and that he himself did not know how to play one, although to do so had once been the fondest wish of his youth.

A form was staggering in the twilight. A small animal followed behind. The lieutenant narrowed his eyes and steadied himself against the table edge. The weaving form shaped itself into Captain Haddock, and the animal bringing up the rear, Snowy. The captain slowed down as he approached the mother and child. He shoved his hand into the pocket of his blazer and withdrew a fistful of coins and bills. These he tossed gently on the blanket by the woman's side. She thanked him.

"Think nothing of it, dear fellow," Haddock answered.

How fortunate he is, thought dos Amantes, to have found the bottle made just for him.

The woman called out another thanks to her benefactor, who had progressed some way up the hill.

"Don't trouble yourself, mate," the captain bellowed back. "Our gizzards need warming these mountain nights. Take your medicine or whatever, as you please."

Dos Amantes sat alone in the darkness of the patio. A gleaming full moon sparked the row of little glasses. The waiter came out and, on seeing the officer, hurriedly withdrew. He reappeared some minutes later, carrying an oil lamp and a plate.

"The sandwich is for you to eat and the lamp for you to eat by," the waiter said gently. "One requires food and illumination," he added, obviously relishing the sentiment.

"It is a kindness of you to do this, Diego, and I esteem you for it. Perhaps you may one day write poetry and join a place of honor beside our greatest poet, Vallejo. It's good that, 'food and illumination.' "

"Thank you, Lieutenant. I know that you read much and are sensible of things of value."

"A foreign revolutionary once called for bread and land. But if you have land, you shall have bread. I like your 'food and illumination' better, for with light we may better see the path to our unfolding destinies, and so we may better conduct ourselves along the trying route. It would not be good if our revolution went the way of many others. We are a gentle people, are we not, Diego? And we should not be made mad

with desires of dark roads that promise to lead—someday—
to light. No, let us have illumination light the whole course
of our road so that we may stop from time to time and look
about us and learn where are the ditches and where the bogs
and where our path detours to side trails of excess and murder, and we must have light to see what those walking in
advance of us are doing—have they donned beguiling new
uniforms, custom-made, and weighted their proud chests
with decorations just newly created by themselves as adorn-
ments of self-love and notice of their superior rights?—and
we must have sufficient light to see far behind us to those
struggling rearward—are they still on the same path with us,
or have they faltered and fallen asleep from boredom or hard
work, or are they injured by the journey and thus requiring
our aid and our tenderness, for not all are able to march at
the same rate?—and we shall require illumination to see our
enemies, who would snipe at us and who would otherwise
set upon our ruin."

"Forgive me," interrupted the waiter, "but right now I
think you need a big light to find your way home."

To go home. That was a poor idea. Not home, to that
lonely room, his temporary barrack, he was not in the mood
for that, not with all this warmth still in him and the need
to play a guitar deep into the night. But he would take an
evening stroll so that the crisp air and the aroma of the moon-
soaked earth might refresh him. And then he would see what
was left of the night and what he might make of it, though
he knew that finally he would return to his room and there
alone in his narrow, hard bed he would smoke cigarettes and
listen to the radio.

The night was friendly and allowed him to feel himself
part of the world, or at least close to it. There was still—and

perhaps ever would be—much absent and much that eluded him. All about him people seemed linked to one another, and they spoke to the point of their being, while he, bachelor, soldier, revolutionary, Indian, was discontinuous and vague. Suppose he went to a café and ordered a hot chocolate and a man beside him also ordered the same. That man or any person would say, "I'll have a hot chocolate," or, "Let me have a hot chocolate," or some such manner of asking, and that would be that. But for him the request would be charged with strange things. Who is the "I" who asks for this chocolate—is it the same man who thought he wanted this stuff three minutes before? And then there was the matter of voice. His own voice sounded far away from him, a ventriloquist's projection. Sometimes he thought to turn about and find where that strange voice was coming from. To be forever outside oneself, that was no small matter, not unless you had many lives and could keep searching for that other self in the time to come or in the time that had just passed, supposing, that is, that the voice asking for cocoa wasn't too far ahead of you, dying before you could catch up with it, dying some-place on a rainy day, a heap in a little puddle, a heap of voice.

Suddenly there was a voice. Dos Amantes looked about. There was nobody. Yet now he was certain that he had heard a voice and that it was not his other voice since he himself had not spoken aloud. This new voice, then, must be one that comes and goes at its own will.

It would be good to go to sleep and let those voices travel where they would. Enough of voices and enough of talk. To sit on some smooth rock was everything. And then, perhaps, once in a while, when a fit big enough to deserve attention swept over him, he would make noises at the moon, little clicking sounds, and then, to surprise it further, let out a long, full, deep, mad howl. He'd see that moon smile a different smile when he got through with it this evening: a smile turned around on a painted cheese.

"Let us have illumination light all the way of our road," the voice was now saying very clearly. "Yes, we must try, Lieutenant." It was Tintin speaking. And in fact, it was Tintin himself there, not five paces before him, standing serenely, his arms crossed, his head slightly elevated toward the moon. "For who else shall illumine the dark regions of our hearts for us if not we ourselves? And without this benignly critical light how may we investigate our hearts and learn its pitiful fear of all the things it knows? Yes, the light of this illumination must be gentle, for the soul must not be made frightened but must be coaxed gently to emerge from the undercave of its dark hollow like a jaguar of no dreadful purpose.

"As for now, Lieutenant, there is much about you I wish to learn. How those of your race came to these mountains and with what intent. Come! Let's find a spot where the air is clear. And when it grows too cold, let us make a fire and leave that remaining portion of the cold night to chill itself. Speak, Lieutenant, in whatever voice you hear."

—————— Chapter XIV ——————

[Later that night.]

They were at table again. Herr Peeperkorn had cajoled and bribed the waiters into setting up a special spread of appetizers for himself and his guests. For all but Captain Haddock, who, still alarmed by Tintin's behavior and words that morning, was lying in his bed, drinking whiskey directly from the bottle. Fatigued from the day's long walk and hot debate among Machu Picchu's stone ruins, they made a sorry table. Lieutenant dos Amantes stared at the cuffs of his military tunic and occasionally plucked a thread from their frayed edges; Clavdia mechanically disemboweled the hard rolls she had arranged before her in a row; the two antagonists, still brooding over the words said and unspoken during that morning's touristical expedition, were jotting notes to use for future encounters, Naptha in his Florentine leather pad, Settembrini in his cardboard ledger.

Tintin fidgeted. His eyes ranged over the small dining room and took in the polished silverware gleaming on the newly set tables. He glanced out the window and studied the contours of the moon-draped hump of Machu Picchu, and finally his gaze rested on Clavdia, his vision blurring and returning to focus and blurring again. He drew his hand to his eyes and remained in that silent attitude until the cataract broke loose.

"I grow weary of the young," bellowed Peeperkorn, sharply snapping off the cap of a beer bottle and giving it a vicious flick across the table.

"Youth is all careless dispersion," he continued, "for youth knows not itself but only its own passionate energy, restless to run off with whatever novelty and adventure pass its way. Motion contains all meaning for the young, and even a moment lavished on simple reflection is considered a small dying. Thus youth hates acorns and all manner of seeds, for those imply futurity and slow growth over slow time, the unfolding of a great organic form over soft and harsh seasons, and youth would devour acorns on the spot rather than plant and nurture them, greedy as youth is for the taste of the moment and heedless of the life they—these seeds and acorns, I mean—may someday spring. Youth reckons the future as the zone of the never. But in you, my dear young Tintin, I sense a miracle, for you are quick motion embodied, yet motion in carriage with consciousness, representing the mentally and physically active life of a young sleuth as you do. Or is it sluther? Which is correct here? What is the clean one called who tracks down the crimes of others?"

"Don't let that worry you, Peeperkorn," Clavdia said, flashing Tintin a smile, her fingers squeezing the pits from a quartered orange. "As long as you stay on your side of the fence, what need to know Tintin's professional call?"

"Why, I thank you, sir, or it seems I should thank you," Tintin answered, averting his eyes from Clavdia's, "though I must say I feel this consciousness of mine, which you speak of, is the rag-and-bone-shop sort, the odds and ends, the trimmings and remainders of a strangely cut cloth."

"Motion and consciousness, I was saying, rarely combine with youth," Peeperkorn continued, "as I so well know from the lessons of mine own. Ah, hear me! Lessons, lessons, this mountain air breeds them. A mountain of lessons, a lesson of mountains. Motion, I was saying. Yes, in my youth I derided the athletic life, all things sportish and associated with the outdoors, with muscles and agility and exercise. I deemed these endeavors and activities suitable for inferior minds and generally mediocre types, for mules of all variety. Somehow, in my early training, my formal education included, I received the notion from those I most admired—my intellectual mentors, in short—that physical effort of all sort—and especially those of the recreational cast—was better left to those whose lives were destined for base things. Then, to make matters brief"—here went up ill-concealed sighs from the lieutenant and Clavdia—"I found, in my virile twenties—in the twenty-second spring of those years, to be exact—that while the athletic life held no thrills, the intellectual or mental life depressed me. Or should I say that I found it depressing since in all justice, the mental life, in the abstract, does not care whether it does or does not depress anyone. Actually the depression came at a later phase or stage, for at first I felt only a lassitude and fatigue with the mental life. I suppose I passed my youth in the amateur fashion common to certain youths born to a gracious life, to the luxury, calm, and voluptuousness of my generation—never mind which precisely—of European bourgeoisie who estivated on the North Sea or Atlantic coast rather than the Mediterranean or by placid Alpine lakes rather than along the lagoons and grand hotels of Venice. Commonplace was my youth, although it seemed uncommon to me then, praising in myself those very qualities of indolence (some call it laziness) and passivity, sincere recoil from all productive exertion, which my parents, my father especially, found repugnant. I imagined myself at that time something of a dandy, an aesthete, a flaneur, a very precious fellow, you know, never realizing for a moment that in this posture I was playing a role played by so many others before me, a role earlier generations had enacted with originality and daring, never realizing that my generation were blurred reproductions of the originals.

"My operation, if you will, was simple: I rose late, well after the household had set about its business for the day. My father was out among his enterprises, small but profitable factories—paper mills and textiles, high-class progressive capitalism, if you allow me that distinction, for out of some loyalty to the memory of my dear father, I would give distinction to that which he himself prided in defining, the differences among the various forms of capitalist enterprise, the various goods and services which it produced. He would, it's fair to say, have considered it beneath him to manufacture arms and explosives, weapons of any kind or of any of those articles causing discomfort or misery or destruction to either its purchaser or those harmed by the said article. I'm growing thirsty. But to continue.

"Of habit I rose late, as I recall just mentioning, taking my *petit déjeuner,* as we termed it, having a penchant, as many northerners do, for phrases French and of Latin origin generally."

"I'll go mad with these digressions. Have you no discretion, no structure? These kind people will presently drop like gassed flies!"

"Correct, just, my dear Clavdia, you bring proportion to this discourse, and try I shall and will to bring the matter more to tow. Rising late, as I say, to the general discomfort of the household, I breakfasted, and usually in my *robe de chambre,* and perused the daily papers, for I had a great fondness for them then, the more vulgar the journal the better, the most vulgar the best. Topics of national and international concern were of no interest to me, but ah! the back pages, the lists of marriages and engagement announcements and obituaries, the employment advertisements, the inventories of apartments for rent, the reports of sordid crimes, these were matters to occupy my entire morning, the little that remained of it, that is, for when I left the table, it was usually the forward side of noon. Others, men and women in factories and in shops and offices, had been at their tasks several hours and were already consumed with fatigue and despair, their grim hearts, as a seaman friend once said, grimly set against the world."

"Just so," interjected the lieutenant, "the wretched and the alienated on whose shoulders you rose in the morning to sip your coffee."

"Would you have preferred that he had chained himself to a factory wheel or to the sour leg of an office desk?" Clavdia asked. "You men are so silly with all your pieties and theories. Why must you interfere with the world as it is, has been, will be? I'm sure your Indians, Lieutenant, are less concerned than you are with their own well-being."

"I doubt that's so, madame. But we of the revolution wish only to let them live as they did before others meddled with and uprooted their ways. Our ways, I should say, since I am of them and was raised among them by my grandfather, and I know very well what we wish. But I fear it may be too late. . . . How many TV antennas do you see rising from the shanties of the poor? They are the lightning rods for the bolts of new miseries sent us by outsiders."

"Never mind, my dear lieutenant," Naptha said reassuringly, "those electronic waves and images cannot injure your people's souls. The soul that is pure is inviolate and cannot be tampered with, as I'm certain you know."

"Pure souls, how few, yet we have one among us, an incorruptible, a natural spirit, a blond elf. Wouldn't you concur, Monsieur Tintin?"

"I suppose you mean me, Mademoiselle Clavdia. And I'm not sure in what spirit I'm to take your observation. For such terms as elf and elfin, elfish and elflike, while descriptive of size and perhaps personal bearing and manner, surely cannot be applied to me since possessed with a soul, I cannot be called a creature that has none, for technically speaking, elves do lack such ineffable components."

"Etymologically and mythically correct and well phrased, my friend," said Settembrini, "but you must admit, granted you have a soul, that you have managed to maintain a certain youthfulness that I suspect Madame Clavdia associates with purity and innocence."

"Thank you, sir, but I find these attributions somewhat condescending and off the mark. In my line of work I have often succeeded by cultivating and exercising not innocence but guile and disguise, subterfuge and duplicity, for when dealing with malefactors and the criminal sensibility, one must, I'm sad to say, be something of a criminal oneself. I do hope, however, that my soul has remained uncorrupted and that I shall always strive for the good."

"Don't be cross, Monsieur Tintin, it's simply that you are so refreshing, so *stimulating*," said Peeperkorn.

"Perhaps I shall be less so as I mature—should that process ever apply itself to me."

"Naturally, and then," Peeperkorn added, "as you mature, you'll come to appreciate less brash pursuits, less stimulating escapades. You might acquire, for example, a taste for collecting what adults consider appreciable goods, *Deuxième Empire* painting and furniture, as an instance."

"I detest Second Empire," said Tintin tartly. "No change of fashion wind shall ever reconcile me to the goods of that epoch, its ostentation fit only for the mentality of the bourgeois regime that spawned it, though I confess that unlike truth, taste is largely a matter of cultural moment, the blossoming of myriad factors not determined by any intrinsic or immutable aesthetic law."

Tintin's eyes gleamed for a moment, his cheeks flushing. He put his small hand to his forehead as if to feel his temperature.

"Excuse me, I really don't know what I was saying just then."

"You spoke with such authority! Such power! Wonderful words," Clavdia said.

"I wonder why, since I don't understand all that I propounded. Heavens! I feel another fit coming over me. Well, yes, in fact, Madame Clavdia, I know there is in all art regardless of the original motive of its creation—religious, political, or personal—a certain quality that distinguishes one work from the other as a work of art, and one may, though not *all* may, recognize this quality. A work of art emanates its aesthetic presence—"

"An ancient and conservative argument," chimed in Settembrini, "one with its roots in Plato, and revived most recently by British art circles of the early twentieth century."

"*Sta'zitto!*" commanded Tintin in a hiss. "*Zitto. Non parlo con te. Non impicciarti degli affari degli altri.*"

"*Ma io voglio parlare,*" began the Italian, amazed to hear Tintin speak in his own gentle tongue, yet offended by the youth's brusque, insulting tone and manner.

"Oh, do forgive me, Signor Settembrini," implored Tintin. "I really don't know what's come over me these last days. I'm in a whirl of changes."

"Then," thundered Peeperkorn, "how warm the world, how snug the nice fit of self, the carpeted parlors of winter nights, the lamps glowing, the red fire in the hearth, a small blaze of scented wood, a pot of tea by my side, an Algerian briar between my teeth, a book—bound in green vellum— of poems by Mallarmé resting on the green robe covering my warm lap . . . no need ever to stir myself into the cold night, into the world, where some, the ice forming about their heels, slept under bridges and on benches of tram shelters, where others, huddling in cafés, were soon to be evicted into the drunken streets. Not for me the poorhouse (lights out at nine) and the wickered iron cages of stone prisons, no illumination there after the natural death of the day, 'cept for the luminous sheen of despair from out one's eyes.

"I did not stir generally, but I must not forget those winter nights spent at the opera, my own box, the *couchette* for naps at intermission or for lovemaking behind the drawn curtain and locked door—those *couchettes* still exist in the Paris Opera House, if I'm not mistaken—my large basket of wines and meaty provisions for entertaining oneself (and a friend or two) during an especially fatiguing recitative. . . . It's of the insular charms of winter, I speak, but I must not neglect to mention the spring, *la primavera, le printemps,* for me the ripe melon of the seasons, *the* season of all my joys, the spring wines of Austria, the spring cherries of Tuscany, the yellow chanterelle mushrooms of Provence, the truffle omelets for breakfast downed with a Pouilly-Fumé while I sat on my petite terrace overlooking the Luxembourg Gardens, all these joys were but the appetizers, the *vorspeis*, the antipasto of spring. Bring back those years!

"Let's start at the Louvre, where I began my active day, a
visit, say, to the Rubens salon after breakfast, among the
satyrs and the nymphs—the little chubby folds of skin about
the waist, tumescent plums amorously strewn on folded
thighs. Then lunch with a friend, of whom I had tons those
days; it's so simple to have friends when one always calls for
l'addition and foots the bill. By afternoon I had covered the
bookstalls and shops and some of the art galleries, where I
was known and well treated as a collector of prints practically
unmarketable to all save me, for I had in those days a special
passion for Dutch prints, torture scenes of the Protestant
martyrs, the market for which I understand has grown considerably since that time.

"The evenings I leave to your imagination. Sufficient to
say that I have always had a need for the company of women,
and fortunately, Venus, Eros, or whoever it is who looks
after these matters, always seemed well disposed to me in
that particular moist channel of affairs—love, I mean. I had
a predilection then (which remains with me even now,
though in an attenuated form, as I'm sure you will note) for
women who do not speak much—the mutes, my friends
would say—but who are, in short, beautiful or, at the min-
imum, radiantly attractive. What do you talk about with these
women? my friends asked, assuming that I required in all
human intercourse the mental, the intellectual, the prattle of
art and books and theater so fashionable, especially today,
between the sexes. By the heavens! A woman should be
designed for beauty, not for function; a racing boat, not a
hauling barge. Oh, how I was taken in those days by elegance
and beauty, by the lustrous hair and the splendid coif, the
pouty red mouth and the trim figure, yes, trim and, how
else to say, the firm-breasted, the complete and self-devoted
narcissist woman who spent her day between the coiffeur and

the pedicurist, the leg waxer and the manicurist, the dress-maker and the shoemaker, the masseuse—"

Clavdia screamed. Little pots of jam and half-filled cups of coffee spun and careened to the floor.

"Talc, talc," cried Settembrini through the door leading to the kitchen.

"Oh, my dear, dear woman!" exclaimed Naptha, mindless of the coffee and milk dripping from the edges of the table to his lap. "What has brought you to this?"

"That he should go on, that you all sit here and *let* him go on like this, that you smile and nod your heads and butter his rolls and pour his coffee while he breaks reason with his aimless, pointless, insolent inventions! He's mocking us, can't you detect that, even you, there, great child sleuth, do you need more clues to uncover his plot? Can't you see that he would keep us here until evening, until the following dawn and even later with these tales, his giant fictions?"

"But, Madame Clavdia," Tintin protested, "he's so fas-cinating; I'm sure we all find him fascinating, do we not, gentlemen? Why, his mind is an enchantment, one learns so much."

"Indeed, to learn his calumnies and lies about women—how transcendental! You imbeciles. Stay, then, his table of dupes, and let him bugger you."

Embarrassment holds the table, holds it even as Clavdia, casting a last scornful look at the silent group, leaves, the metal taps of her high-heeled shoes clicking like furious castanets.

The table remains silent, fixed, except for Tintin, who half rises to avert Clavdia's flight. A voice finally breaks the silence.

"How strange of me not to have noticed that I've been a boring fool, tormenting you with my chatter," Peeperkorn said contritely. "Gentlemen, it needed only a word to stop me, I assure you. Let me apologize and beg your pardon. Yet all may be for the best, this departure of our beloved friend, I mean, her presence being a barrier to the natural flow of the little story I wished to recite, had wished, that is, for naturally, this story must wait its turn, should it ever come again, for a more receptive audience."

"But I'm certain I speak for the others in asking you to continue, implore you," Tintin said.

"How kind, how generous and courteous of you gentlemen. But indeed, I have been truant to the task, a good story needs pith and synthesis, crystallization and compression, the skills I patently lack, to produce the desired effect."

"Well," said Naptha, after a gloomy pause, "I suppose we've come to admire the narrator so much that we are indifferent to his mode of narration—wouldn't you agree, Settembrini?"

"Courtesy demands no less," Settembrini concurred. "But courtesy apart, I am interested in this historical capsule of decadence, having experienced it only through the literature of the period, the usual route beginning with Huysmans and Wilde and D'Annunzio and ending, in its virulent form, in the blood-soaked trenches of Verdun. All those green carnations, that dandified youth, hacked down in full effete flower by the scythe of the Great War."

"Well, then, since I'm pressed to continue," Peeperkorn said, "let me further describe the life I knew in my manhood. To ask whether I had ever a care for the means by which I was able to entertain myself so richly is not to know the disposition of the rich who come by their money through other's hands—my father's, in this case, as I have already outlined. Money there was, and money there seemed ever to be, not that I ever once touched actual currency, for my father's factotum took care of that. I merely had the *statements*, the *bills*—I could hardly bring myself to say the word in those days, it seemed truly vulgar—sent off to the one who arranged everything invisibly. Never once did I ask myself where my life course was leading me, for I thought, simply, that I would pursue the road ahead wherever it went. Profession I had none, nor skills nor trade. Naturally I was never one to twist a screw or steam a hat or shuffle a loaf into an oven. It was long before understood I would never enter the management of my father's various enterprises, my father wisely having decided I was unfit for business and would only bring the whole structure to ruin before his death. He was content to pension me off for a lifetime, content, that is, after the initial and unduly protracted period of dismay on realizing I was what I indeed seemed, a self-indulgent, indolent, ambitionless lad, amiable and perhaps intelligent, but a good-for-nothing nonetheless.

"You may imagine the shock when I received the news that my father, in his full strength and oaken maturity, had gone bankrupt. How, you ask, how did a man so conservative and sound, so renowned for his diligence and husbandry come to that? We search for causes, and well may we search, but I, who then knew less of economics than I do now, understood only one thing: that I was, at one stroke, shuttled into a world that, now that I was penniless, cared little for my polite manners and my splendidly tailored clothes, my fastidious tastes—cared little, in sum, for *me*."

"Good Señor," the lieutenant said, "it is not against you personally that I say this but for the lesson you provide us: that capitalism deserts its own children, is indifferent to all, and raises some with the same turn of the wheel that it casts down others. I'm sure you tasted a bit of want and hunger, for I'm certain that is how the tale usually goes."

"Well, Lieutenant, having read novels and seen films about these sorts of things, the rich profligate abandoned by his sycophants, tossed out by the landlord and reviled by the concierge, scorned by his tailor, a pariah at his club, having been thus forewarned of the practical consequences of failure, I expected no less. And thus I immediately and silently gave all the slip, leaving behind, without a word, my furniture, clothes, leaving behind all who knew me rather than embarrass those who, seeing me in such neediness, would need to invent pretexts for quitting me.

"This, I thought, was wise. I stole out of Paris and went home, such as it was, for in the meanwhile, my father had sold our estate to pay his debtors, never enough to pay all, naturally, and I found my parents in a boardinghouse. It would have been hard, I thought, for a man even stronger than I to adjust to the sight of those two so effaced from their old lives and selves. Papa had grown portly, his cheeks puffy like little soft walnuts, and Mama, that once-robust, nay, *stout* matron, now had become a bone. Penury had quite reversed their physiognomies and their dispositions as well. Where Papa was formally austere and conservative, he was now jolly, making light of his circumstances, of his fall, so to speak. 'The sun shines as brightly on the windows of the poorhouse as it does on the windows of the mansion!' he exclaimed, after greeting me. Yes, Papa, I remember thinking, but the rich have many more windows and beautiful vistas. Mama could not even bring herself to smile on seeing me. She hid her tears badly, and I went to kiss them from her gaunt cheeks.

"She looked at me as if to say, 'Ah, you poor and innocent and spoiled boy, little do you understand what you have in store for you.' Well, she was right, of course. But I might as well have said the same to her, for little did she know during those affluent years of her and her husband's life that the economic ax would descend, and was she any better prepared to fend off its blow than I? Naturally not, but she imagined my future worse than hers by virtue of my utter lack of ambition or skill, for in those days, as I may have mentioned, I could not sew a button or fry an egg, nor did I ever wish to learn these arts . . . and, as for ambition, well, I imagine I've described well enough what little desire I had to pursue all else but studied idleness—a busy enough occupation but hardly adequate to win remuneration in the trade-offs of the human marketplace.

"Above all the question: What of myself could I sell? My good manners? My fine taste in gloves and custom-made shirts? What would that lead to but a clerkship in one of the various haberdashers where I formally had been a customer. Nonsense! No one there would have me. And imagine my having to serve an acquaintance: 'This way to the hat counter, sir.' No, that route was closed. What then else? Sell my body perhaps. Women, I must say at once, were never interested in me that way—not even in my youth, I mean. No, always I was the one who paid, who had to buy. Not my lot to become the lover of a woman who would sell her last diamond to keep her man cozy in bed and at large to enjoy all the enjoyable things of urbane society. And all the rich women I knew actually seemed content in the company of their handsome nephews or, let us say, those men who are the nephews of all women.

"So there we were, this little transformed trio, worthless to the world and, except for a few kind, futile words and feeble pulls at the worn heartstrings of mutual affections, worthless to one another as well.

"This was my first lesson in the ways of terminal family love, and I learned it well, for from that day forth I never wished to, nor did I ever again, set eyes on either of my progenitors. Brand me spoiled and selfish and cruel, yet I am not any of these regarding progenitors in the world at large. The lesson must be learned, the sooner the better for all involved: When love of any kind has outlived its feeling and usefulness and assumed the form of habit or obligation, it is time to move on, to cast off from the mooring, as the captain might say, and sail, sail away. Should I have stayed there in that rooming house to share their fate? Me? Drift out among the unkind streets of my city, trolling for little bits of things to carry home? 'Here! Mama and Papa, here! My ancient and strange dears, for the sake of the life you gave me and the goods and services you gladly provided me, I bring you this small change, the coins of my labor. And now let us set out the dish of porridge and open the skimpy tin of lean sardines, salted and oiled . . . and here, a knot of stringy carrots, a slice or two of mulish salami.' Never mind. Let's end that, quite.

"The idea for my salvation came to me just as my mother entered her third tear fest and my father his fifth hysteric grin. Actually the idea must have been inspired by their routine, for did not these physical manifestations of their misery speak for a translation from one idiom to another? My father's grimaces were the muscular and fleshly translation of what otherwise would have been sounds and words—and how many more of my parents' corporal signals of loss and grief need I witness before realizing the path of my own escape and survival? 'Translate.' The word, in its imperative form, rose up from my deep-most depths. Peeperkorn of the several tongues at service to the paying world.

"So then I was gone; no kisses and good-byes, no wasting of time once I knew I was bound for deliverance. Off to find my livelihood, if not my fortune. I started right that day by walking into the offices of the Mondex, SA, and asking for a certain Herr Raiss (whom I knew only by name), the man recently selected to direct the largest of all consortia in Asia and Africa and South America. Consortium of what? you may ask. Of anything, I answer, of rubber and sisal and cocoa plantations, and mines of tin and bauxite, and all such items whose importance one never notices unless one trades or traffics in them, and yes, this very man whom I had asked to see, sending my card across the table of one of his front-office minions, was the director of all, and yes, you guessed it, after some minutes I am directly invited to Herr Raiss's chamber while others are still cooling their sturdy heels in the waiting room.

"Those waiting others are no less than high dignitaries and ministers and the like, for to get even as far as his main office antechamber required you be of considerable substance, but I march through and am escorted courteously into his office— entirely Second Empire furniture and ornaments and desks, a little museum of Second Empire, come to think of it. Before I could utter a word, a young man of about my age rose from his desk and greeted me with such effusiveness that I was certain he had the wrong person in mind. 'My dear, dear Peeperkorn, at last I have the pleasure of meeting you again.' My mind raced. Who but who was this man who could possibly make life easier for me? Where, in heaven's name, where did we meet, if ever we met?

" 'Heard that you have quit Paris. Are you to stay here with us now for a while?'

" 'No. Just traveling through.'

" 'Naturally this is none of my affair, but I've always been so *curious* about you and . . . well, since you've popped into my office just like that, I thought you might not be too affronted by my directness. On the way to where, may I ask, my dear Peeperkorn? Now that you are flattened—if I hear correctly—where shall you go?'

"So the news of my bad fortune had preceded my own arrival home. So much for my hopes of posing as a man for whom employment was the whimsical aspiration of a rich eccentric. Who the devil was this man? So overriding was this question that I gladly would have forgone my job application, so to speak, in order to resolve it. This man, this stranger of immense power had, for some reason, decided to toy with me, so thought I, while he, with the greatest show of solicitude, continued to play out his game.

" 'Where shall I go? Herr Raiss, let me tell you: to the edges of the world on foot so long as I learn exactly how you know me since I, I'm afraid, haven't a notion of who you may be.'

" 'Peeperkorn, Peeperkorn, I'm not offended, positively not, for why should you have recalled our meeting when I was only one among a group of our countrymen whom Herr Bruckner introduced to you in the Café Voltaire one late winter afternoon when you were discoursing on the virtues of the art of the Second Empire—this some three years ago, when nothing would have distinguished me to merit your attention, because three years ago, when we met, I was even less an entity, a personage, so to say, than now, when my position, not my personality, I must confess, brings me into social and human dimension?'

" 'How you efface yourself, Herr Raiss.'

" 'I allow myself this self-denigration, but I know you are aware that I do this to charm you and set you at ease, for most others who come before me tremble with servile anxiety and all manner of obsequious sycophancy, which, needless to say, as a wise administrator, I encourage. I have cut off most all the acquaintances of my youth and university days for fear they may perpetrate some act or word of some familiarity that my current position cannot sustain or tolerate, but you, Peeperkorn, you who have in some measure changed my life, deserve better treatment.'

" 'How fortunate for me, Herr Raiss,' I said. 'Now would you allay my intense curiosity and tell of our meeting and how it changed your life, as you claim?'

"Herr Raiss and I settled ourselves back in great leather chairs before a huge fireplace; lunch was brought, and consumed, and over the Davidoff's and vintage brandy I heard the following story:

" 'I descend from a line of professional people,' began Herr Raiss. 'My father was a renowned gynecologist, the queen's in fact; my mother, a curator in our museum of natural history, her specialty, the termites of Peru and Chile. So engrossed in their careers and scientific interests were these parents of mine that when, on occasion, they surfaced from their labors to find me in their lap, so to speak, incapable of parenthood as they were, they brushed me from said lap and called for this or that servant or household minion to deliver me to the appropriate chamber—the bedroom mostly— where I was, with the aid of some books and educational toys, expected to ripen, unseen, into full maturity, at which point I would join the ranks of some respectable profession and engage my life on terms resembling their own. Steadiness is all! The most exotic thing my father ever did was to get drunk at a party in honor of the queen's birthday and en route home tell my mother—in a delirium of giggles and high glee—that termites, in his estimation, were the silliest creatures invented by God. My mother did not speak to him for a week, but the transgression was forgiven, and they went along their steady ways soon after. I was destined, in short, for such high-flung paths of passion. But as you shall see, I rebelled and became a rebel.

" 'And now I shall skip an amount of years and bring myself to the doorsteps of the university, which steps I neither trod to ascend nor trod to descend. In short, I skipped this opportunity to advance myself and to satisfy my parents. Perhaps this new Viennese science would explain my shirking of a higher education as a revenge against my hypereducated parents, whom by this stage in my life I presumably would have or should have detested, and the proponents of this science would be in some part correct, for detest them I did, but not for their negligence of me when a child or for their benign and distinctly algid treatment of me during my adolescence, but for reasons I shall not enter into here, and as for education and learning, why, I *revered* these, in spite of their being the trademarks, so to speak, of my parents' whole being, so I would not likely have denied myself the education open to me merely to do these parents spiritual injury.

" 'Why I did not enter the university I shall no longer speak of, and I wish that you, Herr Peeperkorn, would not now or for that matter ever in the future, should you know me in that tense, raise that issue. And thus I drifted, cast off by my own hand, my heart grimly set against the world, my shoulders loaded with big chips, as the Americans say, oh! angry I was for reasons I refuse to divulge at the present time, and thus I wandered through Europe only to find myself in Paris, eking out a living as a bottle washer and all-around slave of the French, whom I detested and who in turn detested me and were only too glad to heap on me all the truly filthy and shitty work that they themselves would have had to do had they not had me, their *garçon*, to perform. "Hey, you there, Hun, mop up the toilet and lick out the bowls while you're at it." The fools.

" 'As for my brothers in misery, solidarity among the oppressed—there is none, or very little, and only among those who wish to make political capital of it. Your true, unselfish solidarity, the consideration of one oppressed person for another, that is the stuff of books penned by guilt-ridden children of the bourgeoisie. And so what was my route, do you then surmise? There in the cellars of the basement of the lowest caves beneath the hotel kitchen proper, where even the busboys spit on you, there I met one even lower than myself, a Chinaman who had passed himself off for a Vietnamese, one of the colonials of the empire, and thus been given the privilege to wash the bottles and dishes and pots and pans alongside me. And didn't I get my revenge! "Slant eyes! You yellow midget, give me a cigarette and light it for me quick before I twist your little coolie chicken neck."

" ' "You needn't go through all that. It really won't help you feel less a slave," this Chinaman said to me with splendid calm and dignity, and in flawless French, I may add. And in truth I was suddenly ashamed of myself for the imbecile and bully I had momentarily allowed myself to become. I had fallen low, just like those who tormented me, my comrades of the steel-counter brushes and the bristling brooms. I sulked and brooded about a long while before getting up the courage to apologize to him. "Yes, of course, think nothing of it," he said, offering me a cigarette. Then we returned to our work, and that was that. Well, to get along with my story, I went on this way for several months, but one day it grew worse, for I was alone. The Chinaman had left for who knows where, South America, I believe he said, and though we never had become friends, we did get along, and he seemed, without his doing anything to make it happen, to calm and reassure me just when I would grow most desperate and

miserable. Well, he was gone, and there I was without a girl
friend, a companion of any sort, alone in the loneliest city of
the world, that's Paris, you know, when you are a foreigner
and poor to boot.'

"Well," Peeperkorn said, "having lived in Paris as a man
of means, well respected and well treated, though a foreigner,
I remained silent; I left him the integrity of his lament, for
that was and would forever remain the Paris of his memories
and his recitations, and then again, there I was in his hands,
*c'est à dire,* waiting to ask him for employment, a position in
some branch of his vast enterprise.

" 'Not that you would understand, having lived in Paris
as you did, and shall again live,' Herr Raiss continued, with
a slight coloring of his cheeks—flushed there by embarrassment or resentment, I did not yet know.

" 'At any rate, I was at the end of the line. I could not
return home, nothing there. And here, I mean, there in Paris,
I was being pulverized day by day. When you work like that,
twelve or fourteen hours a day, you begin to forget you had
a childhood, that you once had parents or friends or a cat
named Nicolino you once loved. You get off work and go
to a café where you know no one, even though you've sat
there week after week; oh, yes, the barman may nod hello,
but that's for his tip—there is not one person you can speak
to about your toothache, say. Every day you start your life
anew since no one knows you from the past; you are simply
a man who comes to take a drink, a coffee. You are no one.

" 'You are nothing, while it gets later and later, and you
stay in that café and have more of what you are drinking, or
you leave for the street and nowhere, or you walk back to
the hotel, to the windowless box of your room. And then,
once there in your room, at eleven o'clock at night when you
are weary and lonely and sick with self-pity, too tired to

masturbate and unable even to think of a thing to excite yourself, because nothing erotic can penetrate the deadweight of exhaustion and sadness, what, then, is there to do but rumple your sheets, clout your pillow, and curse the mother who made you, until you fall into bitter sleep?

" 'One day I emerged from this routine, this habit of staying alive for no reason that I could give myself or anyone else, certain that this day I would resolve once and for all my future course. But as you know, Herr Peeperkorn, such resolutions usually resolve exactly nothing, and somehow I knew that this would be the case even on this day of resolve and hope. It was my day off, a Wednesday, in April, three years ago. I brushed up my old suit and shaved with extra care; my shoes took on a last dying gleam with the aid of my polishings and brushing and rag whacks . . . almost respectable, but not really, for when you've sunk low, you can never surface again the way you once were; nothing short of a radical alteration will bring you back to your class, nothing less than new suits and fresh ties and gleaming shoes and a brand-new job to cap your manner.

" 'Yet I could pass for a distracted student of philosophy out for a stroll, one of those aging, perennial students with small but tidy incomes to keep them anchored to their books and tethered to their scholarly dreams—whom were we reading then? Bergson? Sorel? Fitche? Never mind, I strolled with my heart in my mouth, which is another way of saying you are trying not to look as if you have a prickly spike up your rear. And walking down the Champs-Élysées to the Place de la Concorde, I argued with myself this way: Why should I die when others less worthy live without care, eating at splendid restaurants with impeccably smart women by their elbows, foot to foot under the draped table, drinking bottle after bottle of champagne just for the ordering? Others more swinish than I, more stupid than I live, live to parade little red threads of merit on their dishonest lapels, live to estivate by the edges of great oceans and breezy seas, my God! They live who have the wits of sheep and the charm of slugs while here I am rushing to suicide myself in this disgusting and overpraised river—the Seine, naturally. The French! How they can make whatever little they have appear so marvelous; they believe their own mythomaniac fabrications, and by some virtue of their belief, they make the entire world believe them, too. Oh! How I resented dying in that Seine of theirs, which they venerate as more mysterious than the Nile, more virile than the Amazon, more romantic than the Rhine, and yet there, in that whorish, overtrafficked river of theirs I was about to drown myself because while I loathed others, I also thought I had no right to live, believing that the lowest, most disgusting thing on this earth deserved more solace and joy in one moment than I did in a lifetime, for none was as base and vile and stupid and wicked and filthy and *smelly* as I.

" 'Let me decompose, let me be fish's meat, or let this unasked-for self serve the world in some wholesome manner or, short of serving it, let me, who feel more abject than a flake from a waiter's comb, let this hopeless animal, me, simply cease. This was the ambivalent state of mind when I had crossed the Pont Royal and stood or leaned, rather, against the stonework of the Quai Voltaire. In a moment the Seine would have me, another name added to its roster of the self-abandoned, another meaty meal for eels and river rats. I started to slide myself over the stoneworks, slowly sliding as if a sack of grain inching down a balustrade.

" 'Suddenly I felt a hand on my shoulder, and turning about, I was saluted with immense warmth by a man I at once recognized as a former classmate, one who had gone on to the university, as was expected of him, while I had gone on to the very life I was now faintheartedly preparing to leave. We spoke. He tried not to make the disparity of our situations appear more poignant than in fact it was, while I took great and perverse pains to tell him every detail of my miserable situation—all this over lunch, which my friend most delicately assured me was his treat. How he put up with me I can't imagine. When I asked how he had been spending the years I had not seen him, he attempted to minimize his achievements and successes, while I pressed on him every sordid detail of my subterranean life in Paris. Why he persevered with me I have no idea—Christian charity, masochism, stupidity, boredom—but so consistent was he in attempting to maintain my self-respect that after some while I grew contrite and let down my pose and confessed that at twenty-five I was a failure, that I was *truly* miserable, and that the malignant fruits of rebellion were now growing from out my ears. And in this penitent and vulnerable mood we went, my friend and I, for a long, silent walk to digest this lunch and to absorb, each in his way, the meaning and the future of this encounter of unequals.

" 'After several turns we came at last to the Café Voltaire and stopped to have a final chat over cigarettes, a farewell drink. A table exploded as we entered. You, Herr Peeperkorn, rose and warmly opened your arms to my friend, who returned your greeting no less cordially. You were at your usual five o'clock table, as you later explained, with your circle.

" ' "My circle, I mean that literally, since I term those in my circle whoever circumscribes me at table," you said without a trace of irony or joking. At first I looked for some sign from my friend assuring me that you were a fool and an absolute idiot, but detecting none, I sat squeezed beside you as you had indicated after making much to-do about my friend and the circumstances that had brought him to Paris. You asked several questions of me, too, happy to discover a compatriot, as you called me, and one who looked as though he might become your companion, so alert and so profound did I seem to you, so sympathetic, as you declared several times to the table during the course of the several coffees we shared with you and your circle, although nothing of note or substance had passed my lips to give you any indication of what qualities I might or might not in fact possess.'

" 'Why, how good of you to remember that, Herr Raiss. Rest assured that I must have meant that sincerely or I would never have spoken those sentiments, but I'm still afraid I don't know what to make of it since I can't remember ever seeing you again.'

" 'Never until this moment.'

" 'But then how flattering your memory of that encounter.'

" 'Ah, yes, you *still* do not remember, you have no recollection, then, of your topic of discourse?'

"Well, here I was stuck, and here I thought it best to make my stand, for I felt that what passed from that moment on had to be or appear to be the most frank and candid of utterances—on my part at least.

" 'Well, sir, in truth I do not recall my topic of discourse, and I'm finding even greater trouble in recalling you or your friend whose parents are friends of my parents. In fact, at the risk of appearing bizarre, I'm almost at the point of accusing you of perpetrating a kind of hoax on me, and I would think so had I any idea of what would motivate you to do such a thing.'

" 'My dear, dear Peeperkorn,' he said with the utmost show of concern, ' "hoax," a "joke"—I should be offended or think you mad, yet I understand from your point of view, yes, very clearly how, why you might think such things. In my gratitude and joy in seeing you in these fortunate circumstances I have burdened you with details unessential to this narrative.'

" 'Fortunate for you,' I allowed myself to say a bit tartly, but so intent was he on his own evocation of the past, of our encounter, of who knows what that the comment merely disappeared, as if never made.

" 'Let me say directly,' the young director of companies continued, 'that as the saucers mounted on our table that afternoon three years ago, so, too, my intense excitement at your words describing the universe, especially the art of the Second Empire. Never had I heard history so lucidly and fascinatingly presented. From your lips I learned that what I had thought merely as a decoration, as a frill of life—art, I mean—is bound tightly to the everyday concerns of society and that at the base of these concerns is power, not merely money, and that money is but a branch to the trunk of the tree of power, and the effect of your discourse was to wash away for that afternoon, and many days following, the painful self-pity and depression that had possessed me for months.

" 'And more, I began, perhaps for the first time, to care about elevating myself from my base spiritual and economic station and to think of ways I might start to climb, perhaps even to ascend, to success and power. Something prompted me to consider a reconciliation with my parents as the right beginning, and I was not far from wrong, for when I returned home (I quit the hotel and returned home on the first train), I recanted my obdurate, willful mismanagement of my life and threw myself on whatever kindness was left in them to aid me. They were not sentimental people, nor had they ever shown much love for me on any occasion, and this moment was no exception. But fortunately they were not vindictive persons, neither was bent on making the usual charges and recriminations, there were none of the "we told you so's"—and they did not enlist themselves, as some parents gladly would, in the drama of the return of the prodigal son.

" ' "In what way may we best be of service to you?" my father asked, finally.

" ' "Help me to find some employment leading to a career. Some employment not menial and somewhat worthy of my intelligence, for I do think you have sufficient respect for my brains to know that I may be of use to some firm or governmental office."

" 'Within three days I began my visits to those who opened their doors to me because of my father's solicitations. So eminent a man as he could help pave the way for my entrance into the office of this or that influential esteemed personage, but for all the kindness and respect tendered me in the various offices and reception rooms I entered, I soon realized that there was nothing but courtesy to my father behind it. I was of no use, none even for a clerkship. I had no skills of any sort, excepting those of a kitchen drudge, and no one was about to hire this untested and, by reputation, wayward youth merely out of respect for my father. Presently it grew clear that even with the best of intentions and hopes for a new start, the world was not there waiting to minister assistance and opportunity simply for my asking. Goodwill and my promise of industry and application were not enough out there in the world, where all but exchanges for profit count for very little and where good breeding and manners count for even less (unless, of course, one is a waiter at some exquisite restaurant). Thus rejected, I racked my naïve and untested brains in hopes of finding a route neither I nor my parents had considered.

" 'Frankly, I thought of a life of crime, not that I had

actually experienced such a life or understood fully what it entailed, but there was a certain allure to it, especially after suffering rejection and humiliation at the hands of the very class I naturally would have robbed. How often in my imagination did I thrill to my own exploits, my bank robberies, and housebreakings of the homes and the kidnappings of the very persons who had seen fit to dismiss my application into their service, who had shut the doors to the warm hallways of the middle class. Well, finally, attractive as it was, I did not take the criminal path.

" 'Low, very low, the last on my father's list of people to see, and thus someone who, by the time I got around to visiting him represented for me just another futile and humiliating interview, was Herr Mack, a man my father had not been in contact with for several years, a man whom I suspect my father did not have much regard for, since it seemed he was no more than a wealthy, simple, self-made man in the import and export business. My father had saved his daughter from dying by operating in time, and there seemed nothing to lose, after all, in trying to discover whether the man had kept the memory of his gratitude intact. My letter went to him, his to me designating a day and hour of appointment, but all this perfectly polite on his part, nothing more than "I shall be pleased to meet you at my office." Polite with a shade of the gruff actually.

" 'Herr Mack's office was housed in one of the shabbier buildings of a shabby district hard by the railroad terminus. I expected his office to match the edifice and environs in their soiled and stale dustiness. Not even the vaults of the Paris hotel I worked in had depressed me as much as the waiting room of that import and export business. I wanted to turn and run, but I was sinking so fast into a great sadness and depression and self-disgust that I couldn't bring my body to move. Here was the final end of my youth, my intelligence, my bright green eyes. And now the last and worst to come as the office door opened and I beheld a smallish and balding fellow in his sixties, a kind, ruddy face, a benevolent smile, and all this only made me feel worse, a faster sinking into the collapsing shaft of myself, for now I imagined he might employ me out of some sense of obligation to my father, employ me at anything, and then what would I do for heaven's sake?

" 'For I could not refuse employment, yet this place, that kind face seemed more suffocating than death by pressing— oh, please! Take those stones off my chest! And so I entered his private chamber and there received the first of my several shocks: The furnishings and decor were as splendid as the waiting room and entrance were squalid. And more, they were wholly made up of objects and furniture from France's Second Empire. I said nothing at first but left myself to discuss the matters at hand. Presently it turned out that Herr Mack, like all those who had preceded him, was in no way ready to do more for me than what he was at that moment doing, giving me the courtesy of some few minutes in order to tell me directly that indeed, decent fellow that I appeared to be, and surely one as worthy as the recommender himself (and be sure to give the most cordial greetings to said person), there was no position in any capacity that he might propose at the moment.

" 'My face clearly brightened. Clearly he was not insensitive to the meaning of this suddenly sparkling illumination and with measured, calm voice, terrible in its absolute neutrality, added, "My debt to my benefactor never implied obligation to his offspring."

" ' "Perfectly correct, sir, and grateful I am, too," I said, "but I'd rather die than work in a place such as this. And I am also grateful for the chance to meet at least one of my father's acquaintances who showed his true colors and let down all these civilized pretenses of interest in my welfare. And dear sir, not that you could have a hint of understanding of the things you live among here, grateful I am for the rare chance of seeing such high-quality examples of such and such and not to mention—"

" ' "You are one of the very few who even know what these things are. Most who visit here think they're knick-knacks I've picked up randomly at the junk shops. Then again, in my line of business there're not many who *would* understand the difference between ordinary nineteenth-century junk and these, may I say, great treasures."

" 'And then I repeated to him almost verbatim what you, Herr Peeperkorn, had said in the café, repeated that disquisition on art that had interested me so deeply as to send me to the museums and antiquarians and libraries to learn more, an investigation that further confirmed for me that I had to alter the terms of my life contract.

" ' "Some art," I expounded, "seems to have proceeded from spiritual impulses in the creator, the motive a kind of religious longing—that is, that sentiment which aspires to an act of homage to the transcendent. Thus the paintings of Cézanne, whose mounds of apples are arrangements on the secular side of this religious impulse, expressed in its purest form. Cézanne does not require factors of anecdote and narrative to manifest the spiritual, and Giotto, who does use these factors, is spiritual despite them. To say it another way, Cézanne might just as well have painted scenes from Christian mythology and Giotto painted bourgeois apples; the aesthetic result would have been the same, an art that intuits the metaphysical geometry and is thus the highest form of art.

" ' "Is the art of the Second Empire spiritual in the sense

we speak of Cézanne and Giotto? No, the opposite. It is an art that galvanizes the great moments of materialist cultures, an art expressive of the most comfortable and happy times known in the Western bourgeois world.

" ' "Second Empire art does not waste itself on social homilies, and it is truly democratic in its frank appeal to the broadest spectrum of a culture that equates the amount of labor, the expense, uniqueness, and rarity of materials as the true measure of a work's value—that is, its cost. The more ivory, the more gold inlay, the more precious and semiprecious stones larding a marble-top dressing table, the better. It is an art by and for a class that knew how to take its pleasures, an art celebrating a class that as yet did not whine away its power in bemoaning the very power, daring, and vulgar rapacity that afforded it the pleasures and luxuries of which we speak. Second Empire bourgeoisie did not chew its own entrails in self-loathing for the comforts it enjoyed at the expense of others—its colonial serfs and domestic hired hands. It did not feel the need to apologize for exploitation, dominion, imperialism. The working class and communards of 1871 tried to destroy this culture, but this culture did not, of itself, wish to commit suicide. Pure it was that epoch, as pure as its art." '

" 'And these were my words, you say?' I asked the young director of companies.

" 'Almost word for word, I assure you. The very words that had so sparked my imagination.'

" 'And what was the result, then, of this little speech, quoted, as you claim, from my lips?'

" 'Do not think that was your entire address on the subject. There was much more, and the rest that I have omitted is the real substance of the matter. I cited him only your preface. At any rate, this was the "result" as you call it:

" 'Gorged with pride, with self-satisfaction at my own boldness and effrontery before this man and all that he so unwittingly represented and that I had come to revere—power and capital and money—I was about to leave.

" 'But a change had come over Herr Mack. Where before he had been polite and curt, he now was gentle and solicitous, his diction direct but smooth. Even his rigid, stiff-necked bearing had altered, his body relaxing, till he even seemed shorter than when I first had entered his chamber.

" ' "Well, there's more to you than you present on first delivery; more brains and more mental experience. When I first laid eyes on you, I sensed a vain, spoiled lad, a silly-headed one at that. I don't know how you came upon your ideas, but they fit mine and are the skeleton of my philosophy of life, business, and society. I work here among the artifacts of my class. They are, of course, ugly, but they are the genuine artifacts of a time and a society that knew the value of a minute lost and a minute used, when a man of intelligence, industry, and force might still alter the raw face of this globe and leave his name on an iron bridge spanning the upper Seine or the lower Congo or found a sunny orphanage whence issued healthy striplings fit for the cash-and-carry conduct of this negotiating world."

" 'How to explain that this rough-looking man had within him a mind and character of great fineness and imagination, that his personal appearance and his public facade were guises assumed to ward off the eyes of the curious and the attention of those who habitually pursue the rich and forceful; he was a gentleman of considerable depth and breadth of culture. All this and more, as I was later to learn, was Herr Mack, my benefactor, my patron, my second father soon to be.

" 'But for the moment he allowed himself the declaration of his admiration for my little—your little—speech, admiring most that passage treating the absurdity of guilt in those with power, and in a distant yet courteous manner, he interrogated me on my past, my hopes and plans for a future. Finding in me that balance of revolt and desperation, eagerness and determination, the desire to master obstacles, he offered me the position of his personal secretary, which offer, needless to say, I immediately accepted. Within a brief time I learned the business, and earned Herr Mack's trust and, do I dare even add, his affection. And why not? I found him greater than I had imagined in the initial stage of our professional relationship. I lived in order to do his work, and this devotion didn't go unappreciated. He entrusted me with greater and greater responsibilities until I was brought to the position you now find me, the director general of Mondex International SA.'

" 'Most deserved, I'm sure. You and your enterprise have journeyed high into realms that must have once seemed unattainable. And is it because of you that this humble import-export enterprise of Herr Mack's has entered such empyreal realms?'

" 'Your irony is unmerited and unwarranted, Herr Peeperkorn, yet I still feel well disposed toward you, sufficiently so to come to the point as concerns you and your visit here.'

" 'You are gracious,' I said sincerely, taken aback by his civility toward me, 'and I do expect you will understand that I was unprepared for an encounter of this nature. Moreover, I confess I feel defensive, considering I'm in your presence as a candidate for your favor, a position of inferiority I never before have experienced with anyone.'

" 'This tale, meant to allay, seems only to have disquieted you,' Herr Raiss said. 'I should have said simply: "Shall I, who am in your debt, do no less for you than what was done for me by my benefactor?" *I* shall give you the chance you deserve and need, so not another word on *that* matter except to outline the range of your future activities for us.' "

"That's quite a tale, a saga of metamorphosis and achievement, but I notice, if I may be so bold," interjected Settembrini, "that you neglect to mention that this equitable treatment received by your downcast friend, and yours through him, was occasioned by the facts of your bourgeois parentage; neither you nor he would have had the opportunity to rise once fallen had you had no connections, no old school cravat, as the British would say, to provide you with the necessary ladder on which to scale."

Before Peeperkorn could reply—he had paused to quench his thirst with a nearby jug of beer—Tintin asked: "And what became of you, Herr Peeperkorn? What were your future activities with this enterprise?"

"Pray, Herr Peeperkorn, do not leave us hungry now," added Naptha, "just when we've swallowed your stimulating appetizer."

"By no means shall I leave you famished," bellowed the narrator, "but with so heavy a *vorspeis* in your guts, I'm sure you've space only for an additional morsel or two."

"Room enough, sir, *adelante*. I, too, desire to learn the conclusion to this bourgeois, utopian fable. Then perhaps one day I shall return the favor and relate a history of my people and how *they* manage their lives."

"Kind of you, Señor Lieutenant, yet surely the history of the oppressed is universal and, from my perspective, to be perfectly honest, uniform. There is so little glory or glamour in the history of sufferers; what occasional allure there might be," Peeperkorn said gravely, "is so lost in the crushing mass of details of exploitation and injustice as to hold no more than fifteen minutes of the reader's attention. The German peasants of 1524 no sooner picked up their scythes than Luther's knights—his patrons—speared them like ripe tomatoes in the field. Indians beg for corn and are sent bullets to eat instead. What does all that prove but the ignominy of the cruel and the powerless of the wretched? Better those tales of human spirit rising, examples of the mighty collective soul witnessed in individual achievements."

"I hold nothing against your fable, señor," the lieutenant said, "and I shall attend you with interest, for it is not every day an Indian from these mountains learns from the mouths of his enemies how class interests superseded all other human ties."

"Not quite fair of you," Naptha commented gently. "Isn't this more a tale of the attractions of the human mind, of intellectual and aesthetic affinities, the magnetism, of one delicate and tasteful soul to another? Herr Mack, as you remember, did not favor this youth for reasons of class or even *personal* obligation; he was taken by the youth's ability to glimpse the underpinnings of beauty. The sympathy of like minds is foremost in this tale."

"But no such sympathy would have mattered had Herr Mack not perceived a quality to be exploited to his own advantage! *Sapristi!*" Settembrini exclaimed. "In this youth Herr Mack had found the perfect minion, with whose soul and class he was in harmony."

"Let us hear out the rest of Herr Peeperkorn's story," Tintin pleaded.

"With your good wishes, I shall continue," Peeperkorn said, giving Tintin a little bow with his head.

"One morning I met Herr Mack himself, who, on the strength of my friend's recommendation, gave me a hearty handshake, a steely look in the eyes and a 'welcome aboard.' So I came on board, but not to the upper, plusher cabins, so to speak, or to the flagship of the fleet. I was sent out into the wide sea on a leaky little boat of which I was the sole master, navigator, and seaman. No sunny office in a major European capital, no long business lunches, no agreeable secretary to screen my calls while I read the newspaper or cut out little paper dollies, feet on desk; in short, I was provided with none of the urbane comforts and ease of the managerial class.

"No matter. This was no mere import–export business I set to work for, no, sir. Import profits and export dreams, more like it. I was its chief export, shipped out to the Americas to look after its various interlocking companies, corporations, ranches, farms, plantations, mines, shops even. I was the inspector general, very general, as you well see.

"Off I went, tramping down from Tijuana to the tip of Tierra del Fuego, up the Andes and through the Amazon basin. Across prairies and pampas I went by rail and car and boat and burro. The Americas were my district, a territory where you made a pile of money in a month of sweat and lost it in a night of gambling and women, where the Southern Cross blinked out in its torrid message in the hot sky— WELCOME TO SOUTH AMERICA, CONTINENT OF CONTRASTS AND ROMANCE—not my kind of territory at first, hard and gritty and tough on the liver for a pure white man, yet once it got in your blood, you couldn't get over it even if you lived five lives more, because that macumba magic gets under the skin, those nights on the sands of the copacabana with the jet black mountains at your back and that purple ocean before your eyes, savage and sexy like a jaguar prowling for porterhouse steaks in a summer rain, or out there on the grassy flatness they call the pampas, under the stars so close down to a man he can touch 'em with his fingertips, so close he'd have to crawl on his belly just to get to his blanket spaced between sky and earth. . . . Well, sirs, a man gets to love it so much it near spoils 'im for any other life. Now I don't say it's all

the same everywhere, 'cause it ain't, but even when you're
staying over in some little town like Chapingo or Belém or
Dos Cruses, you get to feel that you could stick it out ifen
you had to, why, that's the beauty of the whole thing down
there, any little place would do you fine, 'cause, like I say,
it's living in your blood, and you can't return to them anemic
places where they *oui-oui* and *merci bien* you to sickness.

"I was on the move. Just got my foot in Belo Horizonte
and looked over the diamond cutting when I had to move
out again to oversee our coffee and rubber plantations, flying,
you know, in a little single-propeller—no bigger than a sleepy
mosquito, and getting closer and closer to up north and the
creamy Andes. Nets at night over your bunk and plenty of
quinine through the day. Well, sirs, soon enough I was feeling
at home in the working world. And I was getting sharp and
*careful;* having to talk to managers and engineers 'bout production levels and the like keeps you wide-awake and on the
lookout! My body toughened with all that travel and hard
driving in the great outdoors; yes, sir, I tightened up that
pudgy and softy frame, and soon even my little butterball
cheeks sank away, my face now the color of smoked hickory
and the texture of a cowpoke from Archer City, Texas, and
so lean and muscular that each chew sent sexy ripples up and
down the jaw and around these blue eyes, for my eyes were
blue then.

"Amazing how from one month to another I had shed the
old self and all of Europe with it, and by God, I became a
man. Good-bye, then, Kurfürstendamm and Unter den Lin-
den and farewell, Champs-Élysées and Boulevard St. Ger-
main, and I really hope never to see you again, Via della
Croce, Piazza Navona, and Via Veneto, so long once and for
all, you mincing, corrupt, and jaded streets of Europe what's
caught sleeping sickness and will never recover, 'cause here

I am steaming it along the upper Paraná en route to Corumbá and then by shanks' mare and horse hoof to Cahloo territory, where the cattle multiplied on our little twenty-five-thousand-acre spread like amoebas on a sea of jelly and broth, and now I'm entraining to Puna de Atacama, to take a little peek at how we're doing in the way of our mineral digs. Our hefty extractions of wolfram and vanadium, mica and talc, tin and antimony are yielding about one hundred eighty-eight thousand four hundred thirty-four metric ton a year, but after spending a week up in those Andean veins, I see that we can produce as much as eight thousand metric tons a year more by just switching from handcart to mule cart from the mine to the train. The trick there was to get feed for those mules, and I found just the way.

"Well, the long and short is I was happy. I'd found that a man is no more than the work he loves and that when you got that kinda work, just get down on your knees and thank the Lord for each living moment. Don't mean to boast, but pretty soon I got high respect from the folks back at home office and even a copy of a letter from Herr Mack boasting of my productivity on all fronts of our operations. By and by, after a few years, Mack and Raiss let me share in the profits in my district, a tiny share, but enough to give me some surplus income, which I invested in a little island smack in the Amazon, where I planted rubber trees and tobacco, coffee and cocoa, and drew a high yield of balata gum and oil from the juicy kernels of the babassu palm, which I rafted down to Pará.

"Money enough and land to cultivate, soon enough you find it cultivates you and roots you like just another tree! Well, who wanted to move? Not I. Companionship? Enough native plumage landed in my branches to keep me content from time to time. Some even nested with me temporarily, but that's another matter. Attachments, cohabitation, marriage, monogamy, children, to my mind, in those days, equaled death of the soul, and the body, too. I had not yet met Madame, you see, and still knew nothing of the joys of union—soul twins, profound that experience, very.

"Then one day out there on my little island I took sick. It was the certain end of me 'cause they got little nameless germs out there floating in that jungle stream that once they've bitten you, it's time to think over your life and make peace with your maker. So I was lying there in my wide rosewood bed, my flesh dripping over my aching bones, my hair falling out in colossal clumps (it's grown back since), my eyes melting in their hot sockets. It was good-bye, little island, and farewell, great large world, but I had known some years or so of happiness, and I couldn't altogether discount those times in Paris when I enjoyed myself, not knowing a life more grand and vital, more personal existed. When you dawdle over sherbets and kir at boulevard cafés, you think the world's winnowed down to your select table and your habitual corner . . . *n'est-ce pas?*

"Well, there's no discussion and no appeal. I had to leave, against my wishes, a life I had not as yet completely tasted and fully plumbed. Some do not mind, some welcome and beg for the end of all vital emanations from their body, so miserable, so hard, so deprived their lives. But for me the fun was just starting, the big loneliness of life ready to be filled with new moments of adventure and challenge; the man or woman narrowed to the small scope of routine he or she has not chosen, whose each new day is but the echo and mirror of the last, has little cause, so thought I, to wish to keep breathing. To have lived one dull day is to have lived them all. But I, in the amplitude of youth and power and money, could live ten times over and never feel the sate of repetition or the gloom of staleness.

"All of you speak of humanity's call for fairness, to make the tall average out with the short, the rich with the poor, the bright with the dull. Yes, at the bottom of the barren well of the long argument there is only that, the grading down of the highest to create the inconspicuous average, and I, too, think it will one day happen, the great races and the great noble cultures will bastardize and mix with the shiftless and noisy peoples, those for whom quietude is torment and who must each instant fill silence with noise or rave in the pain of their own emptiness, this uniform, ugly world will arrive in due course, but I there, dying in the lush days of my youth, there among the implements of my thriving farm, the little blue diesel tractor brought piece by piece overland and by steamer, each arrived section a triumph of culture no less great than a Beethoven string quartet, a Cézanne painting, yes, and each acre harvested and each animal birthed in that tropical riot a victory of civilization, and each worker and his family who came to labor and dwell on my busy and happy island, a triumph even greater. Oh! That was the promise of a second tilled Eden wrested from our knowledge of good and evil and thus greater in value than the innocent garden given our original rude and dullard parents, to all this and more—my darling silver fox and my noble Labrador, my pets, my friends—I was saying farewell and was blinking my last longing glance when he arrived, summoned as final resort by the wife of my overseer, a woman whose overbite and soft round shoulders drove me mad, I might add, though without any meaning to this story and to the events succeeding it.

"He arrived, that frail slip of a yellow reed, and he touched me with his long yellow fingers as if touching a dying white monster.

" 'The smell,' he said, 'white people smell so terrible, especially when they die. White cheese lying out too long.'

"And so there I was, a runny Camembert stinking up the bed and house. He had the houseboy spray my fetid room with a perfume made from the essence of crushed camellias, and only then did he return to administer his frisky medicines concocted from boiling the herbs, roots, barks, leaves, and mossy webs he had gathered that very day. I drank the bitter syrup he spooned me and plunged into a long sleep. It was the sleep of life and dreams, and the fevered sleeper knew that this Chinaman's syrup was negotiating for my life with the assassinating bugs and had, by the close of the third day, won my reprieve. Within a week I was alive enough to sit up in bed and eat a proper meal and was strong enough even to receive this Chinaman of mine to my invalid's bedside for breakfast and conversation.

"He was not much for conversation. He had come by, he said, only to take one last look at my condition and be off about his business. And what was his business? He shrugged, twirled about the room, flailing his skinny bare arm, and, from the perfect French he had been speaking, launched into shrill yaps of pidgin English. It struck me like a slap, and I broke out into the first great laugh I had since weeks before my illness, that laugh that steals up and takes your unconscious by surprise, releasing you for a while from whatever misery disease has brought.

" 'Well, sir, that should finish the matter,' he said, speaking again in French as he turned to leave.

" 'Take whatever you want but stay,' I pleaded.

"He paused. There was in fact something he wanted. He was quitting these parts and had delayed his journey because of me, but now he was to resume his long river trip to Belém and would have liked a book for company.

" 'A book? Take my entire library,' I pleaded earnestly, grateful for the chance to repay him. Yes, he was familiar with my library, having slept there from the day of his arrival, but he would never consider depleting it beyond a volume or two, though he would take, on a conditional and provisional basis—to be returned to me by the next traveler to these parts—a copy of Montaigne's *Essais*.

" 'Why, my dear man, Montaigne you shall have, and whoever else of that ilk of pensive men you desire. Name him, and if he is on my shelf—or obtainable through direct order from my bookdealer—he is yours.'

" 'Montaigne will do for this trip, to have him by my side for a while, to remind me how men thought before they fell into degraded times.'

"Ah, there was a theme worthy of several evenings of after-dinner conversations, aided in their flow by fine brandy and rich, moist cigars—and I had these to offer should he wish to stay—but no, he was an adamant Asian, very correct and ironic at once, and finally very irritating with his sense of modest self-assurance, his polite smile so perfect in its stand-offishness, in its contempt for all that was not, and you could be certain, nothing quite was or ever would be, perfect. So, then, that's how it fell out, he leaving and my getting ready to be strong and healthy again and to build my wonderful world.

"Does that satisfy you gentlemen? To know how fortunes are made from dreams and how chance interceded to aid even the most undeserving. Mark your words, for who knows on what ears they adhere and to what use they are made in this world's drafty and public stadium.

"And so now I'm off to my room," Peeperkorn announced. "I feel the need to repose and refresh myself, as do our friends here, judging by their somnambulant, nay, slumbering, attitudes—note, my lad, how Naptha curls himself like a folded guitar and how our companion from the Italian peninsula pillows his head on crooked arm, a picture of the beggar boy napping in a rotting corner of forever dying Naples—yes, I, too, hear Morpheus's song drawing me to the warm sheets of sleep. Young man, I perceive that drowse and fatigue leave no impress upon your smooth features. Resilient youth, elastic heart, bring yourself to my rooms at the hour after dawn, when we may then continue, on newer grounds, to engage our personalities and bridge the distance of our souls."

"It would be an honor to converse with you, if I understand your intentions, sir, but I fear disturbing you from your morning sleep since dawn breaks within the hour."

"Who spoke of rest, my boy? That was the inclination of the moment, a breeze that has come and gone. Presently, then."

# Chapter XV

[An hour after dawn.]

Peeperkorn ushered Tintin into a large, brightly lit room where, with exaggerated flourish, he directed the young man to seat himself in a wicker chair set before a solid French easel. In the interval since their last meeting, Peeperkorn had exchanged his mountain costume for simple coveralls and a coarse linen shirt, open at the throat. While Tintin sat expectantly, the old man slipped on a thick brown tweed jacket leathered at the elbows, and after some moments of searching in his trunk he produced a wide-brimmed straw hat, which he patted affectionately before crowning his head.

"My good-luck hat."

"Are you going for a walk, monsieur?"

"Walk? Why would you think that?"

"Your costume, sir, suggests an out-of-doors atmosphere."

"These are my work clothes," Peeperkorn bellowed, "though naturally I wear them *en plein air* during clement days."

"Are you going to work now?"

"Why, of course. I work every day, and shall until these eyes and hands fail me. Work invigorates, fuels body and spirit."

"I should be leaving then," Tintin said disappointedly.

"Leaving? Nonsense! Remain you must. This is our moment. There is so little I know about you, my dear youth. Of your exploits and adventures, naturally, as does the whole world, but to learn of you and your thoughts, your inmost history, this was my intention in organizing our little tête-à-tête this morning. Oh! Yes. And now, by way of preamble, an introductory note, let's turn to a related matter, my life's passion, my work, about which I ask your opinion and your advice, because I've come to an impasse, one which I believe your judgments and feelings may help me span, being, as you are, wholly honest, wholly *au courant* with the matter at hand, since, as I've learned from your salty companion the greathearted Captain Haddock, you've a taste for painting, if your acquisition of one of the most precious artifacts of contemporary art, that Matisse of yours, I mean, reflects such taste."

"Well, sir, I do like pictures."

"Ah, yes, pictures. But I was thinking more in the line of paintings. I have arranged here, along this wall, as you see, my portable museum of miniatures, uniform-size paintings, scaled-down copies of the original canvases I've executed over the years. I hasten to add that what I shall show you is merely an anthology, a fraction of my total oeuvre; it represents each of my various periods, from the earliest to the very present."

"I'm honored, Monsieur Peeperkorn, yet as to the advice you seek, I'm certainly not qualified to render neither you nor any artist such service."

"Come along then," said Peeperkorn, seemingly oblivious

of the young man's objection. "The exhibition proceeds chronologically from left to right."

The canvases, each the size of a large handkerchief, rested against the base of the wall.

"How do you expect to see them from up here? On your knees!" ordered Peeperkorn.

Tintin obeyed as if on reflex, and in kneeling position he swept his eyes over the span of the sixteen tiny paintings.

For all their differences, each (except for those of the later period, in which the image was not distinguishable) was a painting of women and men, but one face repeated itself in differing contexts and costumes: Clavdia's. It is Clavdia who reclines, nude (except for a narrow black bow about her neck, a tasseled bracelet high on her forearm, a green shoe on her right foot), on a pillowed divan, her face serenely turned to some visitor, or to the painter himself, but almost certainly to the viewer facing the canvas. Behind the divan a thickset black woman in white robes extends a bouquet of flowers, probably a gift just arrived—for they are still wrapped in tissue paper—to this Clavdia, who, for the moment, takes no notice but who will perhaps momentarily turn in acknowledgment of both the black flower-bearer and the flowers.

And the smiling, youthful face of a ballet dancer, her body tilted forward slightly as if bowing to an appreciative audience, also belongs to Clavdia. In the background, other dancers are bathed, as is she, in the warm, burnished glow of the stage lanterns. Dancers whose faces are, on closer look, mere smudges of paint. What warmth, what happiness animate this moment for the performers, who, as Tintin imagines, must soon make their way backstage to change into ordinary garments (thick sweaters and burly cloth coats) and thence leave the theater to cross cold streets and frozen iron bridges.

Here in three-quarter view is Clavdia in blue silk high-necked dress and matching blue bonnet seated in a wicker chair at the seashore. The modeling of the upper body and face is precise, clear, while the cliffs behind her are a blur of autumnal colors, the sea a scumbling of blue and whites. There is a sweetness in her expression, the start of a smile as she looks out beyond the canvas, perhaps to one who has just called her name or voiced some endearment. This idea suggests itself to the enchanted Tintin as he turns to the next painting.

Clavdia, her skin dark cocoa, her long hair shiny black, reaches out for a turquoise-green banana hanging low on a purple stalk girded by an orange snake. About her waist a vermilion cloth falls to her knee, the black nipples of her full, naked breasts glisten, as does the narrow golden halo about her head. Beside her a thin lemon-yellow dog sleeps on a swatch of ocher earth. Smoke rises from palm-frond huts set in jungle clearings. This Clavdia neither smiles nor seems serene; her broad, masklike face is a surrender to blood, to deep pools and waterfalls, to the meat of near-raw fish braised by green sapling fires in early evening.

In the main sketchy, seemingly unfinished, the next painting takes solid form in the handling of the upper torso of the figure, in the modeling of the slightly inclined head. There the planes of the face seem to dovetail into rectangular shapes. It is a middle-aged house-tending Clavdia these shapes suggest. Clavdia of the kitchen, Clavdia of the scalded morning milk and pot of steaming coffee set on her husband's wooden tray. This is the Clavdia who keeps the household accounts and makes the butcher tremble and the maid's eyes tear. Yet, soon, under Tintin's insistent gaze, the domestic face now proposes nothing but the shapes that so subtly compose it.

He was growing dizzy with these sights and reflections, and the small of his back, his knees ached. He thought of rising, but at that very moment Peeperkorn's sharp voice brought him to attention.

"Too much for you? Tiring? At your age! Surely, Madame deserves more of your attention."

"Oh! Sir," cried Tintin, "I'm neither inattentive nor remiss in my affection for you or for Madame."

"Well, rise then. Anxiety makes me gruff. I beg your pardon, my dear boy. So profound is my concern with these efforts that I'm apt to take any hint of less than unswerving interest as lack of approbation, a dismissal of all I've suffered to achieve."

"But they—they are *magnificent!*"

"Do you think so?"

"Stupendous," answered Tintin, genuinely moved.

"Not too eclectic, eh?"

"You at once capture and transcend the original sources; you synthesize and distill; from the old you create the new."

"Your words gratify me, young sir. Quite," the older man interjected. "When all is said, my art so far would not exist at all if those whom you deem my models had not labored before me. But now I must explain that I've reached my crossroads—a momentous occasion. For either I shall continue to travel the route you've here witnessed, a worthy route, culturally wholesome and with honorable precedent, or I shall set forth to take the path to the new, the wholly virgin land, where only I shall have the moral and aesthetic authority to issue passports and visas to those who may wish to follow me there. And this is why I need you. For what is it to have struggled for the discovery of virgin lands only to suspect that others have trod those paths before and perhaps have even built their outposts in the very regions one seeks to claim?"

"I had no idea, sir, that you had such serious interests. . . ."

"And indeed, why should you? To the world and at times even to myself, I am a gluttonous fop, distracted, senile even. That is, in fact, precisely how I wish to be noted, all the better to keep my dwindling energy intact. Show nothing of yourself to the world, my young man, for it is a jealous, vicious place. But I'm sure you know all this; one cannot be a lamb in your trade."

"One cannot neglect the devious side of things, yet I've fared well in this life with captain and dog by my side. No need of guile with them."

"You are fortunate, my boy," Peeperkorn said, falling suddenly into the whisper of an old man, "for obviously you've lost nothing in life. No need, then, to hold tightly to your heart."

At that instant Tintin's heart fluttered. Some dizzying apprehension seized him, and he returned to his seat by the easel. His voice was suddenly muted, distant, the voice of someone about to fall into a heavy sleep: "I think the world an endless seam of pain where loss and gain come around and around again; here the heart and there the mind and ever yet the world to find. When one lives well within one's skin, then all the world's in bloom again, but bloom, too, shrinks to death and nothing, and one's own skin encases mattress stuffing."

Peeperkorn, tenderly: "Count not the cycles of these things; bloom and shrink and nothing be, but feed the heart its fertile springs, grant the mind its wide periphery.

"But you're pale, my lad; I must have taxed you too hard. Yes, sit there awhile, restore yourself. A glass of champagne to brace you, a sip or two of this blond tonic, and you'll be back with us again."

"Thank you, monsieur, but I think some fresh air will help more."

Tintin opened the window, thrust out his head, and inhaled. Blood slowly colored his cheeks; his eyes again focused sharply. In the distance he could discern Clavdia, in her long blue dress, strolling; some indistinct but male form accompanied her. She tossed back her head, as if laughing. Tintin longed to be by her side, to carry her purse, to offer his arm as she stepped over the outcroppings, to help her descend the ancient stone Inca stair, to say amusing things, to amuse her.

"You are wholesome once again! Air is your champagne, I see."

"Quite fit, and ready, with your permission, to examine the rest of your marvelous paintings," said Tintin, resuming his kneeling position on the floor.

"Well, then, consider these last few, the most recent, for here the problem lies."

Tintin inched away from the central paintings to the cluster terminating the exhibition, to come upon Clavdia standing alone on a tropical islet (the vegetation resembling none known to any botanist) in a calm lagoon. A fur cape that is draped about her shoulders falls to her manacled wrists. How more voluptuous and seductive that body as when now topped by a falcon's head. Indeed, in no other painting thus far has Clavdia's form been so beautiful and desirable.

To row across that silent lagoon, to beach boat and alight, to unchain those wrists and feel her grateful embrace, yet perhaps only to have her thrust her rapid beak into his pounding, love-filled heart. Bound and captive she *must* remain, Tintin mused, the words so loud in his mind he feared Peeperkorn might hear them.

Yet in the following painting, unbound, naked, joyous Clavdia wheels with other naked, happy, loose-limbed young men and women in a dance of life. Hand in hand, they spin in ovoid orbit on a field of timeless blue.

He would have remained at this painting had not Peeperkorn's sounds of impatience (or so the young man interpreted those huffs and throat clearings) urged him on.

Her mouth a jagged jack-o-lantern, her wide face seems to fly to the canvas edge, one eye already having left the facial terrain and leaped from its socket to seek an ear. The canvas sputtered and glided with paint. Clavdia, for he could only assume it was she, was the swirls and streaks and drips of yellows, reds, greens, zinc whites.

But in the penultimate canvas Clavdia, or rather the image symbolic of her, was once again restored, her face occupying almost the entire canvas. It is a face boldly outlined, as are all her features, suggesting an enlargement from a cartoon or *bande dessinée;* and no less indicative of that archetype was the "balloon" above her head, embracing in its wavy closed circuit the motto *Non mi toccare.*

The final picture (a mechanical reproduction of a silk screen) was the word "Clavdia," stenciled letters frozen in a flat field of gunmetal gray. The gray letters glistened dully and with what seemed to Tintin a transcendental shimmer.

Tintin rose and thrust his hands into his pockets. Peeperkorn's voice broke the silence.

"There you have it, and there I rest. There on the easel a newly primed canvas, and here, in my imagination, a blank. I've mastered the technique and spirit of every modern movement and every modern artist's modality right to the present, and now I am off on my own, all alone, all me, into future history. But I have a minor problem, which you may help me solve. In short, what shall I paint next?"

"But why ask me?" implored Tintin, drawing his hands from his pockets and clasping them before him.

"You have a strange mannerism there," said Peeperkorn, staring at the youth's hands, "much like a beseeching schoolboy. But it is I who am beseeching, I assure you."

"How shall I answer such a question?"

Peeperkorn paced about the room, turned to the easel, studied the tiny handkerchief-size blank canvas, frowned, smiled at it, caressed its surface, inclined his head toward it, and whispered. He placed his ear close to the canvas as if waiting for a voice to reply, and hearing none or dissatisfied with what he may have heard, he withdrew and once again addressed the youth.

"Why, here is the problem. I have explored all forms of Clavdia in all forms. Will my subject, this Clavdia or my ostensible subject this same Clavdia, be the subject—present, willing, able—of my next work? Will she be there, I ask, to go with me, hand in hand, so to speak, to that land where I shall have sole dominion, issuing there those passports and visas mentioned earlier, or must I, subjectless, terminate my career and retire, with only this small museum to show for all my efforts?"

"I suppose," answered Tintin, more baffled than before, "that I would do anything to aid and satisfy you, to answer your question even. But I know nothing else to say except what says my heart. Yes, yes, *cher maître,* travel where you will, and should you conquer that terrain—of which you speak so beautifully, may I add—grant me a visa there, for I shall be an early applicant."

Peeperkorn, his cheeks flushed, his eyes glowing, regarded the youth for some time, while Tintin stood awkwardly in the center of the room, his hands still clasped before him.

# Chapter XVI

When finally he did speak, Peeperkorn had so mastered himself that in voice and features he once again resembled the affable old charmer of the dinner table.

"This devilish vanity," he said, stepping forward and putting his arm about Tintin's shoulder, "crops up even at my age. Quite ludicrous this vanity of the aged; it is a kind of forgetfulness of our true station to assume, as we often do, that saplings heed the downward fall of ancient oaks, and obviously nothing I've said is clear to you. Your sweet nature touches me and reassures me."

"To be in the orbit of your attention is what I hope," Tintin answered gravely.

"You ask for so little," said Peeperkorn slyly. "Yet it is not an untoward hope. There is so little I know of you, my dear young man. Of your exploits and adventures, naturally, I know as well as any who follows the press, but you and your thoughts, your inmost history, and I quote myself earlier, these were and remain the constant aim of our morning interview, if I may call it that without seeming impersonal."

"I'm unused, sir, to speak this way, not even with the

captain, my life's companion. My natural diffidence, my aversion to examine the personal self—I never read autobiographies and may have missed much in dismissing from my education the great Rousseau or St. Augustine—retards the flow of my response. I wish with all my soul to meet your wish and to share with you what little I know of my small life and thus to win your sympathy and perhaps even your affection."

"Oh, my dear boy, do not wrench yourself. I hate to see you rip against your natural grain. Perhaps some vodka or a jug of champagne would stimulate the flow of your blocked nature."

"Alcoholic drinks! So early?"

"What does the body know of the hour of the day? Is not time merely a human artifice? Is soul not present at all minutes?" inquired Peeperkorn as he handed Tintin a glass of champagne. "Now, then, doesn't that taste good?"

"Yes, sir, it warms me. It feels so grown-up to gulp champagne. It gives me hope of conquering timidity. I think it shall make me voluble and bold. And so boldly, sir, I shall meet your inquiries and boldly I shall examine and reveal my heart."

"Where were you boldly born?"

"In Brussels, I think. I know little of my earliest days."

"And your parents?"

"Both dead, I think. My mother is dead. I never met my father. He may be alive. I remained the same size since the day—the night actually—mother died. It was about that time I began to receive letters from Brussels advising and directing and instructing me toward my various criminal investigations over these years. Somehow these instructions conformed to my youthful dreams of adventure, to my sense of justice, for in all I had read, the world had many wrongdoers, and their elimination would bring our planet some measure of calm and happiness. I set out, alone at first, to rid the world of these persons. *Hélas!* I have learned that wrongdoers are as numerous as the stars.

"But life is long, I reasoned, and what better way to spend it than in action for the good. The captain and the dog my most chief-most comrades, but even in their pleasant and devoted company I have felt lonely and frequently sad. Often I have tried to see the bright side of things and have said to myself that it isn't so bad to be always small and unaffected by things that sway larger human hearts. I have argued this way with the captain. 'It is not a matter of my choosing; I cannot will myself to grow, to sprout hair and elevate my stature, so leave the matter to itself,' I would say.

"But now, *cher maître,* here in these enchanted Inca mountains, a new life seems coming. Startling and wholly new these sensations and feelings. Each hour I discover a change, a deepening of my voice, an increase in height. Yesterday, I'm embarrassed to speak so plainly, I woke in bed to find my penis stiff and tall, rising up like a pole, and I rotated it against the cloth sheet. How good it felt at the root and the top. Snowy leaped upon the bed and followed the movement and pounced. No, no, Snowy, it is me here, not some mouse or snake. And I thrust back the blanket to show him. He was frightened at first and jumped off the bed, but after some moments of hanging back in a corner he returned and looked appraisingly as if to say, 'Now, there, Tintin, see how it is? See how it feels when it comes over me and I'm moved to rush off to find a place to plant my pink shaft.' Of course, I didn't know what Snowy was thinking. But I gave him a hug of sympathy and kinship. 'My dear Snowy,' I said, 'forgive me for having been so unkind and arch with you in the past when you have swayed from duty or from even your

normal stroll beside me to bound away after some lady dog.'
Then, suddenly, I thought I could hear Snowy's thoughts,
his internal dog voice.

"*Ah, Tintin, oh, how much more I love you now. At last you've
entered the human station and joined the rest of your kind, and in
doing so have come closer to knowing me, though beneath you as I
may seem to be in my doggy ways.*

" 'Beneath *me*,' I replied. 'Never! Your nature is fine and
your courage great. But I do not understand how you can
go off after dogs of any and every sort. I've seen you sniff
about stunted and manged strays as well as great elegant
creatures leashed to the most fine, aristocratic hands. Do your
promptings recognize no distinctions, style, rank, beauty?
Or do you simply go about in the catholic lust, a true democracy of uncensored longing?'

"*For me, Tintin, there are only fellow dogs. We dogs do not say
of our kind, 'This one is fat or this one thin; this one is graceful
and this awkward.' We need no aphrodisiac of scene or costume, no
illusion or mystery. When my pinkness emerges, I wish to mount,
to do my doggy plunge without attention to refinements.*

" 'Well, dear Snowy, have you ever loved?'

"*Yes, twice. But I soon learned that love was not for me. Attachments, especially in our detecting trade, cannot bear permanency.
When one has taken up the life of pursuing criminals, as I have
done in following your service, there is little hope of long connection.
Once I thought of leaving you and remaining with a bitch I met in
Madrid. She and I discussed this often in our little strolls along the
Paseo del Prado . . . but I could not forsake you, who would not
understand my disappearing. And how could she abandon her master
to follow me to the derelict back streets where sooner or later we'd
be rounded up and motored to the pound—then, saffron, onions,
and lethal gas? Oh, Tintin, she was the one to snap my castanets!
Those dark eyes of hers, her moist snout, her well-bred aroma!*

" 'Well, Snowy, it seems you, too, are not exempt from valuing appearances and personality although you claim the contrary.'

"*An exceptional case, that one. A sort of sickness came over me, unique for her, too, that malady. Perhaps our long association with humans occasionally gives us dogs strange ideas. At least she thought that. 'Snowy,' she once said, on the corner of a great avenue, 'I'm not certain whether knowing you has ennobled me or debased me, for to feel for you as I do is to feel as a human, and it is not clear whether the human sentiment in these matters is not, in reality, a madness. We canines,' she continued, 'are liable to illness, worms, and infections, the rabies, but it is unnatural to add to them those borrowed from our masters!' She was eloquent, she. And dainty. How gingerly she'd squat, barely touching the ground or pavement on which she'd squirt a lemonade stream. I was ill when we parted, almost wished myself in the boneyard, me always dwelling on her, sniffing the air for a whiff of her. And dreams! Real howlers. I'd wake with tears flooding my eyes. My paws ice cold, my snout dry and stiff as sea tack. España! Tierra del sol y de la señorita* Concetta—*for that was her name—España, the land of my joy and my sadness. And so I am as you see me now, Tintin, restored to my natural being, Snowy once again, despite my bittersweet affliction.'*

"All very illuminating, Tintin, my boy. Decidedly provocative a digression, your speaking to and comprehending your dog, your rising erectile tissue. Formidable. But earlier you were speaking about your mother, I believe."

"Yes, yes. But I remember little of my mother," Tintin said sadly. "She was beautiful, I remember that. Sometimes I would go into her bedroom to watch her dress. It took her so long to dress, but I loved watching her roll up her silk stockings, her robe spread apart, and fasten them, one after the other, to the garter belt hanging flat on her solid white thighs. I'd sit on the bed's edge, watching her brush her long dark hair in the evening before going to a party or a dinner. She'd be soon gone, and I was in bed alone again. I'd often try to wait up for her, to hear her steps at the door and the turning of the latch. I'd hope she would look in so I could pretend she'd woke me, and I'd plead with her to join me in bed and to kiss away my bad dreams."

"Now, now, now," interjected Peeperkorn. "Now we are getting right to the stuff of life, right to your psychic mold, my dear boy. At least some would say that."

"How do you mean?"

"Mean? That you've explained your interest in Clavdia, that you have found again your lost mother."

"But I didn't think of Mademoiselle Clavdia in that way. Not like a mother."

"So you say, and so, I'm sure, you think. But consider, dear youth, that your secret sexual life is awakened, only now, under Clavdia's charming sphere. There is undoubtedly some association you make between this Clavdia and your mother; you were too young, among other considerations, to possess your mother, who, as your brief description indicates, excited your oedipal wish, but now fortunately you have found her again, the mother for whom you've unknowingly longed."

"Pardon me, dear sir, but do you tease me?"

"Not in the least. How else to explain this implausible attraction? I mean, not that Clavdia herself isn't capable of charming *anyone*, but that she should have charmed *you* demands more explanation than the usual."

"But to speak this way of my mother! Surely, if you did not intend to offend me—or did you?—you meant to provoke me in some way."

"No, no. Quite reprehensible of me to dabble in this abject

and amateur psychic sleuthing. Unlike me at all costs. I must have picked up a touch of the psychoanalytic infection during a brief stay in North America—at some lecture or after-dinner conversation, no doubt. God, how virulent this disease and how innocently it must bite one to have gone unfelt until this moment.

"Yet I can't help following this earlier trail of analytic thought. Isn't your mania for chasing wrongdoers, as you term them, a wish to punish your father, whom, I take, you resent for having abandoned your mother, whether through death or desertion . . . it is immaterial? Isn't your wish to punish miscreants the world over prompted by your wish to protect, to win your mother, as if to say, 'All men are not bad, dear Mother, regard me, for example?' And haven't you remained the size you are in order to dwell ever close to your mother, to remain *her* child forever, while rejecting the badness you associate with grown-ups? I shall not be like my father, I shall stay a child. Thus always to be loved, thus never to be wicked, thus, moreover, forever to defeat, forever to replace, forever to vanquish your father, all fathers, all of us grown men—me.

"I should say you stunted yourself by keeping the trigger of your cells locked. And then Clavdia's appearance sprang the psychic spring, sparked the chemical fizzle, and *voilà,* the once-arrested clockwork of your retarded body was propelled into motion, into natural organic time. I may have mixed my metaphors, but you do understand my analysis, even if I have been somewhat flippant, less than candid, jocular even, my remarks to you a subterfuge. I've talked a great deal in my time, so many thoughts and arguments and convictions, so much experience, if you allow me to say, too much experience for one man, too much to reflect on, to absorb, to master. . . . This makes for a tiredness. I'm drawing down

with me the whole of my life. And you, you have suffered
many trials in foreign places. You have suffered even more
greatly the loss of the mother, and your wish for the mother
is a festering disquietude alive in you all the long day. Is not
Clavdia the amniotic fluid in which you long to bathe once
again? Think, Tintin, is not her caress the return of all your
childhood desires now fulfilled? Can she be your mother and
your woman? *Dites-moi, Tintin, mon petit.*"

"I have known her all my life, from the womb, as you
would say. She pulls me where my soul has always been
waiting to visit and to dwell. Now I know, too, that we've
met once before, at Villefranche or Knokke, one of those
places we summered as children. I saw her then, we passed
by at dusk, she holding her father's hand, her eyes the slate
color of the North Sea. I was nine. She, ten, eleven. I remember her now because I remember no other woman as
well excepting my mother.

"*Maître,* I love her, have loved her and shall love her."

"*Moi aussi, mon vieux.* So the question is, What shall we
do? A turn of the dice? A cut of the card? A flip of the coin?
A gentlemen's agreement? A duel? Will you stab me while I
sleep? I mistook you. Not to that new land of hope will you
guide me, but to the precincts of loneliness."

"*Maître,* you break my heart to speak to me thus. I beg
your pardon."

"Because of *that*? Sweet lad, were I to be angry for that,
I would have burst from anger a century ago. Clavdia has
worn holes in more mattresses than could be piled high to
meet these mountains. To be plain, her body—"

"Sir!"

"Her body, I say, has received visitors the world over,
quite international in its hospitality. Hardly a fortnight passes

when some sweaty new tourist has not visited and departed enthralled with its vistas and its culture."

"Calumny, vile and unworthy of you; you blacken yourself with these ugly, jealous words."

"Doesn't it excite you? It does me, my dear boy. Thrilling quite, to know that she returns to me, time and again, after each coupling. Thrilling also to learn the details of her adventures. You, though she has refrained from speaking about you, I'm sure must have to go a long way before making a dent in that person about whom we are speaking.

"Above all, you must understand," said Peeperkorn gravely, "that this woman about whom we speak is *folle*. I say this neither to insult her nor to hurt you, but to caution you, should you be so naïf not to see the evidence for itself, which, if you were wiser, would have been as apparent as the brogues on your feet."

"Again, you demean yourself in demeaning her."

"*Pas de tout*. I inform you of this as mere courtesy, since I understand that you understand nothing of lunatic matters and are preparing yourself for a grand and I hope not too hurtful disenchantment. Let me expand on the subject, for although I recognize you shall neither understand nor believe me, I feel obliged to set out the truth to you in order that I may feel less culpable for whatever befalls you in the future. Let us say, then, that this little lesson is more for my own future benefit than it is for your present good. Be seated, I mean, seat yourself comfortably and firmly, have more drink, a cigar, or if you choose, there's some morphine and needles on the tray beside you."

Tintin said not a word but looked at Peeperkorn with rage and wonderment, wishing he could choose a course of action, wishing that he could remain seated with the demeanor, if not, in fact, the actual feeling, of equanimity or, short of that, that he could rise from his seat and rush to the self-possessed, nay, smug *Senõr mein Herr,* and strangle him until his old man's eyes popped from their sockets. Rage, in fact, was new to him, so new that he wondered at the sensation, half enjoying, as he did, the bursting heat to his blood. The sensation, so novel—though its memory surfaced from a distant dream—so pleasant in its conscious form, almost made him forget the cause, so that when he next heard Peeperkorn's firm, authoritative voice, he had to muster up in himself all the powers of his diffused concentration in order to speak.

"*Folle,* you were saying, crazy and lunatic, she, about whom you and I, but mainly you, were speaking."

"This madperson is, among all, the most mad, most lunatic, most crazy," Peeperkorn said. "That this person, when not in public, that is, when alone with herself or with a lover of long duration for whom the need or desire for maintaining a state of *mystery* and artifice no longer exists—that lover thus relegated to the condition of a lapdog or any other accessory in the furniture of her life—this person about whom we are speaking spends most of her waking hours preening, primping, tweezing, cleaning, washing, bathing, combing herself, spends hours in having her body massaged, her hair cut, coiffed, conditioned, her nails trimmed, shaped, buffed, polished (toenails, too, I must add), and whatever else is done in the manicure procedure, her legs waxed (the most effective means of depilation), leaving her long, long legs and thighs and inner crotch smooth, especially after oiling. Let us add to this particular inventory of *soins de beauté,* her exercise class, lately supervised by one Amedeo Hartshorn, age twenty-three, a Nordic beauty of slender frame and brown, liquidy eyes who spends two hours a day in demonstrating and supervising Madame in the sit-ups and knee bends and torso twists required to keep said Madame in perfect working and aesthetic order.

"I do not count here the vast hours spent from home in the same pursuits—the salons and clinics dedicated to the care of her face, the various mud and herbal concoctions, the electric facial stimulations, the removal of dead dermis tissue and the dermabrasion to give creamy texture and youthful tone, and the silicone injections to smooth out wrinkles about the eyes whenever those aging signs should make so bold as to appear on that perfect face—nor do I speak of those visits to the cosmetic artisans who give no end of time to the contriving of pigments and powders and dull or glossy unguents to enhance and accentuate this or that feature of Madame's countenance, to capture the reflection of this or that tint in her purple eyes at morning, midday, and evening, prepared, of course, to suit whatever latitude and longitude and season Madame's face happens to find itself, for the dim gray light of London in winter requires different eye shading from the harsh, humid glare of Rio in summer. No, and I shall not add the spas to which Madame takes residence to follow for some days or weeks the regimen of hot natural baths, to drink the mineral waters, Karlstadt . . . Marienbad . . . to name a few only that have seen her name inked on the register. Now to the matter of clothes, of costume and the like, firm, firm yourself for this epic inventory—"

"No, I wish to hear no more."

"No more? Would you be content, then, to consider the sum required to propel Madame out for an afternoon promenade and window-shopping expedition on the Rue Faubourg St. Honoré in Paris, say, her coat, sable, dollars beyond dollars, her rings rich and costly, her shoes Delman, her simple dress Chloë, her gloves and scarf Hermès, the limousine and its chauffeur to bring and fetch her back . . . not to mention the stop for lunch, usually at Maxim's—the front room, naturally?

"My inventory does not include the actual purchases, which, on a dull day, a day when Madame is bored by the uniformly mediocre quality of the goods proffered her, may total some thousands of pounds, a mere nothing by her lights, and by mine, too, when compared with the days when luck favors her with the opportunity of buying goods rare and beautiful and without which her life would be impossible, unbearable. May the heavens help me on those days when chauffeur returns home with Madame's items, a vase from the Ming dynasty, an Orientalist painting for only the cost to feed and house a family of four for a year, an eighteenth-century green briefcase from the Rue Bonaparte that shall remain untouched in her closet. Now, you say, this does not make Madame *folle,* and this you may well say, for the pastimes here enumerated would describe half of the bourgeois world of Paris and Milan and perhaps Brussels, but I answer, this represents only a fraction of what is required to keep her from the madhouse, where I admit it would be considerably cheaper to maintain her but where I as well would be deprived of her company. For if Madame is not *occupied,* Madame is crazed most unpleasantly.

"In the course of our cohabitation, our inequitable partnership, Madame has attempted several pursuits in the hopes of giving herself peace of mind, a feeling of worthiness, of purpose, meaning, and well-being, of having a place in the world, of defining herself as an individual apart from her identification with being merely a beautiful woman whose status derives from the man she is with, of allowing her to feel and believe herself an autonomous, integrated personage of standing in the purposeful cosmos: photographer, painter, dancer, poet, novelist, essayist, student of law and philosophy and botany, bricklayer, sculptor, beekeeper, filmmaker, actress, decorator, volunteer social worker."

"*Stop.*"

"Stop, now? When you are just beginning to get the picture, so to speak? No, my dear boy, you must hear the rest, must learn, for example, how once while I was sleeping, she hovered over me, knife in hand, preparing to stab me to death for the simple reason that I was to blame for her misery. Had I not supported her, not pampered her, had I just kicked her in the street, so went her charges, she would have made her way, would have found her Self through hard necessity. I, and only I, was to blame for allowing her such amplitude of play and experiment, thus reducing all her activities to mere hobbies not to be taken seriously by herself or the world at large. That I had indulged her in all these attempts at self-defining activities proved me a weak and selfish fool, for as she insisted, a man authentic in his powers of understanding her and her needs would have sent her off to work, and thus forced her to define herself, or made her bear children—this while the knife wavered over my head.

"A simple incident repeated in various ways over the course of our union, but now let us take an ordinary domestic evening by way of model to this Madame's nature. An evening at home—how rare in itself—dinner and, for want of more illustrious diversion, a game of gin. We play; she is distracted; her eyes vacant, dead, she deals the cards slowly and furiously in turn; she stares at her hand while I patiently and with infinitesimal care attempt not to show my horror at the length of time these cards remain under her dull gaze; she finally plays out the hand and all the following with the same uninterest. Should she lose, she claims I have cheated. Once actually, sure of finding concealed cards, she made me turn my pockets inside out and roll up my sleeves, claiming hysterically that there is no use in playing when she cannot win. Should she be winning, she remains silent, smiling, and from smile to smirk and smirk to guffaws of triumph—guffaws, mind you, and I must pay up *immediately,* cash, no checks, no IOUs—but should she lose, she moans that I take even her little savings or shrugs off the debt since, she reminds me bitterly, the money is mine anyway.

"You are wishing to leave, Mr. Tintin? Stay, and explore with me Madame's activities on the horizontal, on love's platform. She'd make a whore blush with modesty. Thank heaven! Have you yet noticed, for example, that Madame will most gladly put her tongue where a gentleman would not dab his walking stick?"

Tintin, fists clenched, lunged at the speaker, but then, gaining control of himself, he turned to the door.

"Stay, there's more! What I have told you is the simple appetizer of the fulsome main courses yet to come—the body of the menu of her personality."

"You've already fed me enough spoiled dishes, sir. I'm quite poisoned, thank you. What harm did you think I would or could do you that you stirred in your person the muck better left settled? Whatever once drew me to you, the filial impulse, the recognition of your grand personality, the respect for your mighty largess, I now disown. Henceforth all tokens of respect and loyalty are broken; the field is open to all claimants."

# Chapter XVII

[Afternoon, same day.]

Tintin's solitary walk brought him close to the precipice where he had heard Naptha expostulate on the penal codes of the Incas. He halted on seeing Clavdia and Peeperkorn conversing animatedly by the historic and fatal edge. They gave no sign of seeing or hearing him, no indication they were aware of living in this world.

Clavdia shrieked, "We've tried it all before. There is no place on this earth for us, no place where we shall lose each other!"

"My darling, there is so little time left me, what does it matter? Let me finish these years with you."

"Be generous."

"As always, you mean."

"Be generous now. Let me go."

"Is it this boy? There've been other boys, less rare than he, perhaps, but with discernible virtues, I mean, with qualities."

"Cease meandering! Halt! Open your ears to my words! No tricks!"

"Trick? That I adore you! Have adored you since you were a child."

"And I, too, you, even now. But your adoration chains me. Venerate me from a distance. Write me long letters. I shan't be stopped this time. I need my life even more than what in it keeps me fixed to you. I need to live my time!"

"Live it then! Live the paltry themes of your generation. Leave me for your cradles and your bibs, but not a penny of mine shall you have. Where's your freedom then? I disown you. Vanish in rags."

Peeperkorn's words froze in her, and speechless she stood, her body rigid, her position held fast as though by guy wires anchored deeply into the earth.

Tintin watched in disbelief, undecided whether to advance or to retreat, though soon, as if guided by sentient beams, he turned and silently made his way back to the hotel. Once there, he sank into a cane chair on the red veranda.

As the air was growing darker about him, Tintin felt he had reached the end of something familiar, a frequented self from which he was about to part, and in the leaving, there was at first a sadness (farewell to friends at piers, as ship eases out of port; the final turning away from a beloved house), then a nostalgia (the perusing of old snapshots, letters, journals of one's life), then a murky recollection (old men are said to wonder whether they indeed lived the life recollected or ascribed to them, it seeming so far removed from the immediate time in which they live) that he once had been Tintin of Marlinspike, a youth.

Tintin rose from his seat and, giving his body a feline quiver, commenced walking in the direction of the precipice and the humans he had recently left there. Finding the two poised by the precipice, in the exact attitudes and disposition last described, he advanced toward them rapidly. Peeperkorn seemed lost in himself or in his view of the silver-blue river sparkling thousands of feet below. Tintin's eyes met Clavdia's for an instant, and, believing an affinity of desire there, he swung around and lunged toward Peeperkorn, who, about to smile and speak, stepped back and fell into yielding space. Tintin and Clavdia watched him hurtle silently until the tiny form that was his body met the distant earth. Taking her cold hand, Tintin led Clavdia from the cliff. He spoke only once before arriving at the hotel some minutes later, his voice so firm, clear, and deep as to seem wholly new: " 'I wish I could believe we are now forever wedded in guilt and love, but I have the premonition that in this act we instead have severed all bonds mutual to our lives.' "

—————— Chapter XVIII ——————

[Evening of the following day.]

The lieutenant sat at the desk of a police station some miles below the hotel finishing his report—death by accident of one Herr Peeperkorn, who fell to his death, his great corpse cremated, the ashes flung across the ancient ruins and down to the river below—and he would stay the night. Captain Haddock and Snowy had retreated to their room just as Tintin and Clavdia appeared, the captain making much of his need to pack for the morning's departure. Settembrini and Naptha lounged morosely at the band's usual table, but without its full complement. The evening's dinner table, decked though it was with wild mountain flowers and sparkling with water glasses and gleaming silverware, looked funereal. When Tintin and Clavdia joined them, the atmosphere did not visibly improve. Settembrini shrugged his shoulders and opened his hands as if to ask, "Well, what excitement is left now without Peeperkorn to prod us with his dazzling life?" And Naptha, dressed for no apparent reason in a smoking jacket, gazed about the room looking for the absent one who had ruled the board these past days, days that indeed had seemed several years.

"I see there is sorrow here," Tintin said. "It sits at the table."

"Sorrow and vacancy and all manner of sadness there is," Naptha said dolefully.

"Loneliness has taken *mein Herr*'s seat," Settembrini added, but then, as if suddenly struck by the black band about Clavdia's arm, he composed himself, took the woman's hand, and kissed it. "For what little I have and what little I am, I offer you my services at this terrible time."

"And I no less," Naptha said, rising and clicking his heels.

Clavdia nodded her appreciation to the two men and began to speak, but Settembrini's words cut her short. "What does it mean for you to offer anything, Naptha, you who have so much? I grieve the loss of so great a spirit and offer Madame my spiritual aid in some small fraction of recompense for her loss."

"It is selfish and cruel of you to quarrel at this moment of anguish to Madame. I ask you to desist, if there is kindness left you," Tintin said.

"Yes, of course," Settembrini answered ruefully. "My apologies, Madame. Yet to lose *mein Herr* speaks to me of all my losses and of those yet to come, of all the deprivations I have lived and have been made to live," Settembrini continued, transfigured by his urgent misery.

"And you, Naptha, who offers services, offers nothing that cannot be provided by your wealth while I must suffer the humiliation of making a second-class gift, the paltry present of my feelings, the gift of all who are penniless. That this should be my lot, a second-rate life, I, who was born in the image of a prince! A second-rate life. I, who should have dined at the tables of the Farneses, supped with the Duke of Montefeltro in his exquisite court in Urbino, I in the company of poets and philosophers, I, munching sugary pears and grapes fresh from the tame hills. For one who understands quality, anything second-rate is humiliation. I go with cloth coat; you, Naptha, with fur. I must purchase reprints; you, first editions—in original bindings. I travel second class, with children and needy professors on grants, lodging always at the lesser hotels, in rooms without view, sometimes without windows. Breakfast specials, sugared bun, weak coffee, the waiters never frightened or withered by my displeasure, knowing I am only second class, only a cut above them. In your capacious apartment, Naptha, you have guests for tea, a servant producing silver trays of biscuits and moist sandwiches, the dark rims of crust cut away; you invite and are in turn invited; I am the perennial guest with no hospitality to return and thus forever at the rear of the table (and *dare* I not be charming to hostess and her friends, *dare* I contradict or show my boredom, *dare* I not play the ebullient bachelor!). They do not say of me: 'He dresses shabbily because he is eccentric, but in truth he is rich.' Or, 'He is not rich, but he is famous, for something or another.' I am invited to the dinner table, but the host has long forgotten why.

"Alone, all alone. I, who dreamed of beauty and love, who dreamed, as a youth as well as now, of my ideal, my Beatrice, my life, mother and virgin and ravishing *puttana* who wants to be plunged front and back, who would hold me, head on her lap, she in a blue silky gown, her golden hair fanned by the hilly breeze, hold me and caress me and speak lovingly to me, always loving me, always attentive and respectful of my learning and culture, and yet here I am, I, I, who dream of her, ill from longing and deprivation. I cannot bear it, my

dear friends, old and new. Perhaps I am pathetic in my longings, in my vision of beauty and love, *ma sono fatto così!* I am
made this way.

"And you, Naptha, the world is yours, yet you despise it,
not what it refuses you but for what you cannot provide it,
a fair form, handsomeness, beauty."

"To be just," Naptha replied sadly, "we are both somewhat meager."

Clavdia signaled Tintin her readiness to leave. But he stilled
her with a calming movement of his hand.

"No, we are nothing, you ugly, I poor; unloved."

"Loveless."

"Lovelorn, I may add."

"But," Naptha said timidly, "I feel, sometimes, I care for
*you.*"

"And I *you,* at times."

"Most likely I shall never find the Isolde of my dreams,"
Naptha said fiercely, "no such woman seeks me, yet I, too,
have yearned for a love greater than love. Or at the very least
for a companion to scale cliffs over a furious sea at dusk, for
a mate to share a dinner and an evening's concert in winter.
Has not *Brüderschaft* a place in human love? And if I cannot
find an Isolde, may I not find solace in Tristano? In short,
must a quirk of gender keep one—me—from love when
love—or affection, its diminutive form—presents itself, as I
feel, Signor Settembrini, it is currently presenting itself?"

"I, too, feel its presence, and it shames the various un-
pleasantries between us."

"Why, then, we have, if no one else, each other."

"Do we?"

"I shall protect you; you shan't want again."

"Is there enough in your hoard for two? Or must you

dilute your treasures, leaving us to live in less than first-class style?"

"More than enough, a superabundance. I have lived humbly in comparison with what I might, for there was never reason for luxury before," Naptha said.

"You dazzle me. Here, let me butter your toast."

"No butter, my dear, and you must forswear it, too," Naptha said reprovingly. "We have little enough to offer each other without worsening our lot, bad for the arteries, and fattening, you know."

"Nonsense!" roared Tintin in a voice consonant with the recently departed one's. "Faddish slander! Your butter, lard, margarine, olive oil, all the holy brotherhood of unction lubricate the bones and muscle and give an unguent sheen to the crackling skin. Why, these little butter patties are oily eucharist to the dry spirit as well as the dry flesh, quite. I anoint your bread; here, I'll froth your toast with butter. Lovers you shall be, and hearty ones. Let you love robustly, no watery spendings! Settled! May proud Priapus love you. Toast, butter, eat."

"I am so pleased for you both!" Clavdia exclaimed, kissing the two on the cheek. "A reconciliation at last."

Naptha and Settembrini, their eyes shining, left the table shyly, followed by Clavdia, who flashed a distracted smile on Tintin, leaving him alone in the candlelight, his man-size hands folded on the linened table.

# Chapter XIX

[The following day.]

In late afternoon Tintin and Clavdia strolled arm in arm along the grassy trail leading to the summit of the ancient city.

"Come to Marlinspike, live with me. Inseparable and happy. Think now what has opened to us! We shall meet each day as an adventure, never to be bored or sad, always to do as we feel and wish. Clavdia, so few humans have our chances."

"Which ones?"

"To wake in the morning in our broad bed, under Egyptian sheets; to start our hearts to beat in lovemaking—I shall improve and make you happier—then to breakfast (only now do I understand how lovely that): silver trays aglow on the rich wooden table, on which rest Georgian silver forks and knives beside thick linen serviettes; on table and highboy the morning's freshly cut flowers. Before I imagined sharing one with you, to me, all meals were merely necessary intervals that broke the day. Breakfast shall be our most sacred meal, as it is the one that heralds and fuels our each new day together. What would you like? Cold poached salmon with a touch of dill or capers, or perhaps a lighter fare, some spoonfuls of choice caviar between drafts of chilled French champagne? Then coffee, brewed from beans still fresh from the blue, wet hills of Jamaica ... or some other kind of caffeinated beverage should you prefer."

"My little menu, I've had *all* that *all* my life."

"With someone you love and who loves you?"

"With men."

"But all that does not count now. There's never been happiness before. Why fasten the past to our present lips?"

"The past lives in my every cell. Every gesture of my every day."

"Nonsense."

"Nonsense you! A man is his cohered world, all that which has made him his power, his cuff links. A man is where and with whom he dines, the stitch and cut of his shoes, the lines of his luggage."

"You loved me, not my monograms and suspenders."

"And like you still. But we can't make oaks from acorns in one night. My dear Tintin, take what we've had as a present of fortune, for the lovely moment it was. It is unfair to attempt to build on what was so captivating, so fleeting, so spontaneous an impulse. And of course, there is him. Do you think I can cast off his weight like that? Sooner toss an iceberg. And when I do shed him and grief has its end, I *must* live my life anew, with no hint of the tainted past. There's no less affection for you in that, but you can't expect me to begin again with you or with anyone just yet."

"Why not? You break my heart just now I've gotten one. It's cruel of you."

"No recriminations, no regrets. Don't press me, or soon I shall loathe you, as I sometimes did my former guardian, my keeper. Let the future recall us tenderly."

"My God, Clavdia, I can feel it. It's breaking. It's the cliff for me, too, then."

"So be it. I can't and won't stop you. No one person is sufficient, no one person can be all for us for too long. I can't endure any one person too long. Nothing for too long, especially myself."

A condor soared above them in an ever-narrowing spiral, as if winging to some point of infinity in the leaden sky. A chilling cloud passed over Tintin's heart.

"He will fly that way until his lungs burst," Tintin said.

"That's farfetched," Clavdia answered, her voice terse.

"Perhaps, but for that creature it is true; he neither knows nor cares why he aspires so fatally upward, but it is his time to do so."

"And what pretty analogy shall you make from that? Are we being signaled of man's urge for the beyond, the above, the high?"

"Humans long for the everything."

"Quite the philosopher! All this from one who only yesterday was incapable of—"

A sudden gust of wind blew across the trail, taking Clavdia's words away with it to the gorge below.

"I grow to know less and less of yesterdays, Clavdia. 'These roses under my window make no reference to former roses or to better ones; they are for what they are; they exist with God today. There is no time to them. There is simply the rose; it is perfect in every moment of its existence. Before a leaf bud has burst, its whole life acts; in the full-blown flower there is no more; in the leafless root there is no less. Its nature is satisfied, and it satisfies nature in all moments alike. But man postpones or remembers; he does not live in the present, but with reverted eye laments the past, or, heedless of the riches that surround him, stands on tiptoe to foresee the future. He cannot be happy and strong until he too lives with nature in the present, above time.' "

"Above time! Indeed. A gallant speech to direct at me, who is your elder and each day drifting to youth's end. Your mouth grows wiser by the hour, but your heart stays offensively simple."

"Your soul has no age, my Clavdia."

"More pretty speeches. Is this rhetoric the fruit of your new learning?"

"I learn new things each day," Tintin said, his blue eyes darkening.

"Wonderful! You learn all that which is common knowledge to most ordinary men."

"I have had to begin from the naked origins of things, but I soon shall thrust ahead, far beyond the common scope."

"What did you learn today, for instance?"

"That you are discontent down to your marrow."

"Revelation! You're ablaze with perception."

"Clavdia, your scorn wounds me and blurs you in my loving eyes. You grow harsh and hard."

"Because you oppress me. I feel oppressed by you. You were delightful when innocent, someone to play with, a novelty. But you've grown too solemn. I admit you are better-looking now, beautiful, in fact, golden, a man's slim body, your voice mellow, your gestures smooth, but I'm weary of you. I am obscure by nature—though I think I hide it well—and need light, and light men, distance, distraction. If you were a tango dancer or a polo player, you would calm me by your natural indifference to my misery. But you want to protect me—and look at the results—you love me without proper reserve, and I'm growing to dislike you for it."

"And I thought, still think in some dream I had of you,

though that shall perhaps fade, that you were matchless. That while the world, save animals and plants and stones, was murky and plain, you illuminated this shadow earth."

"And I thought," Clavdia said sorrowfully, "often still think in some forgotten dream of ours, that you were intended for me, my cells matched to yours. Well, dream or no, I do care for you yet."

"Then, Clavdia," Tintin pleaded, "let us begin again, a new life together, come—

> *"Contigo mano a mano*
> *busquemos otro llano*
> *busquemos otros montes y otros ríos,*
> *otras valles floridos y sombríos,*
> *donde descanse y siempre pueda verte*
> *ante de ojos míos*
> *sin miedo y sobresalto de perderte."*

"Life has many paths, roads, stations, and we shall emerge and disappear, connect and disconnect, in different guises and moods. We have had our moment, but we have lingered over it too long, have let it ripen into sorrow and distraction, into what we now have become to each other," Clavdia said, her hand caressing Tintin's stricken face.

Tintin "glared at her a moment through the dusk, and the next instant she felt his arms about her and his lips on her own lips. Her kiss was like white lightning, a flash that spread, and spread again, and stayed."

Clavdia felt Tintin's warm tears on her cheek and lips; she felt his soul strain to preserve itself, to remain within him, fearful lest it fly from the youth's parted mouth into her own. She drew back abruptly, leaving him momentarily with his arms partly outstretched, his torso inclined as if preparing to board a train that had unexpectedly shot away.

Seeing him in such stunned solitude, his face careworn, his eyes swollen and red-rimmed, Clavdia felt herself soften, opening to him as a mother would to her own hurt child; she would press him to her breast, stroke him, call him sweet names, she would take him back to the hotel, bathe and feed him, undress and make love to him, she would take him into her tenderly, letting him release his anguish in her pitying embrace. But this impulse, noble and plausible as it first seemed, presently felt too imbued with the murky spirits of self-sacrifice and guilt and thus dangerous to her own safety and need for flight. Tintin would have to fend for himself in this world where human feelings change profoundly and suddenly, and if he broke, it was *he* in his untried soul who broke, but not she, who would return to her separate self once again.

"She turned from the young man, and much as her heart yearned toward him, she would not profane that heavy parting by an embrace or even a pressure of the hand. They parted, in all outward show, as coldly as people part whose whole mutual intercourse has been encircled within a single hour."

Tintin watched Clavdia descend to the hotel, her step slow, her head and shoulders cast downward. He would have pursued her, held her back, attempted, in some way, by argument or further expression of his passion, to win her to him again. But another yet stranger impulse gradually invaded him, displacing momentarily the dark, trembling emptiness in his body with an anguish so deep as to make him reel. He felt his life current deserting him through his mouth and fingertips. He sat himself down on a smooth stone, his head bowed to his chest, his arms locked about himself in tight embrace, eyes shut. He thought he would go to the precipice

where Peeperkorn had hurtled off and take a plunge himself.
"It's the cliff for me, too, then," he heard himself say once
again. It was dark and silent; a single star glowed in the sky.
Tintin attempted to rise, thinking to fling himself off the
precipice, but felt too weak to pursue the effort. He wished
his life would be kind enough simply, and with no exertion
of his own, to cease.

"Stop, life!" he whispered to himself.

Suddenly a voice coming from the earth beneath him answered in mimic: "Stop, life. Listen to this kid, will ya? Stop,
life. That's a good one. Stop, life. Look at this, this guy's
gonna flood us with his little boy's weepy eyes. Hey, cut it
out. You're drenching me with that salty eyewash. Whatsa
matter, big boy, your girl just ditch ya? Stop, life. That's
about the best I heard these last years. Hey, fool, why don't
you get going and blubber on someone else? I'm still trying
to dry out from last week's downpour."

"Everyone, even the earth, has a voice these times," Tintin
answered.

"Shove off, will ya? Go kiss and make up, yeah, and make
out while ya at it. Give her a good one for me, and cut out
the bull. Stop, life! Look, I've seen it all, kiddo. I've been a
regular sex mattress for a couple a million years. Everything's
made it here, snakes, jaguars, rabbits, snails 'n' a zillion tons
a humans, all plowing away like there's no tomorrow. So
where do you come off with all that stuff? You think you're
the first chump ever got creamed by love? Beat it, you're
making me old before my time. STOP LIFE!"

"I don't take to your insolence."

"Well, ain't that tough? Whatta you gonna do, piss on me?
Kick me to pieces? For a smart guy like you you're one dumb
dummy. Take some friendly advice: Shove the sob story,
and find yourself another girl—everyone's dating these days.

A good-looking guy like you shouldn't have himself no trouble. STOP LIFE."

"What you say, however coarsely expressed, is sensible, my friend earth. But what to do? I love and am not loved. I suffer."

"Suffering's unfashionable, kiddo. I know you got a dreamy side, but 'believe me . . . you know not what is requisite for your spiritual growth, seeking, as you do, to keep your soul perpetually in the unwholesome region of remorse. It was needful for you to pass through that dark valley, but it is infinitely dangerous to linger there too long; there is poison in the atmosphere, when we sit down and brood in it. . . . Has there been an unalterable evil in your young life? Then crowd it out with good, or it will lie corrupting there forever, and cause your capacity for better things to partake its noisome corruption!' "

Moved by this advice and the thousand thoughts it bred, Tintin knelt to the earth and fervently kissed the humid soil.

"Now you're getting the point, Tintin. One last word, then, before I leave you, with my blessing. Remember always, 'the soul goes steadily forwards creating a world always before her, and leaving worlds always behind her; she has no dates, nor rites, nor persons, nor specialties, nor men. The soul knows only the soul. All else is idle weeds for her wearing.' Go then, life's wonderful child, take to your vision, and leave all else beside."

Tintin absorbed these words with a sigh, each word penetrating and healing even the darkest reaches of his misery. He need not be alien to himself, provided he took the requisite measures.

He reckoned now that his former self had died, that all he had taken as life, encounters, alliances, tables, the palaver of the street, bore the same relationship as the top of the sea to the life beneath it. He had, all these years, skirted the surface of the water merely; now he would swim and dive and among sharks as well as minnows.

"Henceforth I shall commence each day with START LIFE," Tintin said humbly, the tears in his eyes shed no longer in remorse and grief but in gratitude for the lessening of his pain and for the quickening sense of hope and renewal. He would follow life wherever it led him, even to the sources of its pain and joy; he would live, not as do most men, married to guilt and fear, ill from want of love, dreading time and failure, but with a calm in the certainty of life's plentitude.

Love, he thought, had made him human, had given him reference to the deepest longings of his species; the sorrow of love had triggered his desire for death—the beautiful, good, consoling motherfather, the great, dark purple river— and had transformed him (before it had a chance to break him) into something higher than human, had elevated him among the recluses and the seers, but he had yet to undergo another transformation, one more accelerated and radical than that which he had recently experienced. Mysterious how, by the moment, new sensations, ideas, powers, coursed their way through him; how, even now, Clavdia seemed an intense incident in his intense, compressed history—although he knew that his grief would return time and again.

When Tintin returned to the hotel (the earliest light of morning had spread over the mountains), he found Captain Haddock, blazer rumpled, his face sagging with fatigue, waiting for him on the veranda.

"Worried about you, my boy."

"No need, Captain. Get some rest."

*Something's up,* Snowy thought, raising himself from Haddock's side, *knew it when that sad lady came back alone, her face white as a desert bone. Better stay close by.*

"Too late now for that. We're all leaving for Cuzco on the morning bus, Tintin."

"Without me, my dear friend."

Snowy's ears froze; his little body quivered.

"Thundering castanets! You're going too far."

"Beyond," said Tintin with a slight wave of his hand.

———————— Chapter XX ————————

"I sense I shall never shall see home again, Captain. But you return to Marlinspike, my friend; perhaps I may join you there again one day."

"And Snowy?"

"Goes with you."

"I will miss you, laddie. Perhaps it's all for the best, who knows? You've changed, you're almost my height now, your voice is deep, a man's, you think strange thoughts, and I confess I can't plumb them. No fear, I will tend Marlinspike for you, and wait for you, and keep Snowy's larder filled with bones and biscuits."

"Don't drink too much, Captain. Keep your hatches dry."

"And you, my boy? She's left, you know, in a big black car the size of a yawl. Forget her, there's only sorrow and squalls on that course. My beloved boy, mark the narrows on your charts; I beg you, no dreaming on the night watch."

"Yes, of course. And now it's time to leave, Captain."

Tintin watched Haddock descend the trail to the waiting bus. Snowy turned inquisitively and barked for Tintin to join them.

*What's he up to, hanging back like that? Come along, Tintin, the bus is here, we must be off.*

At last he understood that Tintin was staying behind, and a sudden rush of fear and misery seized him, his bark turning into a whine. Tintin saw Haddock sweep Snowy under his arm, saw the captain's braided blazer sleeve flash in the sun and the little dog's struggling body disappear behind the closing door of the green bus.

In this tumultuous world who knows when one life ends and another begins, when chance and destiny will upturn the solid planking under one's most sturdy shoes? Who knows, Tintin thought, when even the most temperate-zone life will change season and bear hot, flowering trees where cold oaks and pines once stood?

Preceded by two porters in white uniforms, Naptha and Settembrini shuffled arm in arm down the grassy trail. Tintin understood in that comradely splicing of arms that their burning harangues and bitter outpourings, their posturing had at the core only a yearning for love, and at last, after so many deprived, barren years, they had discovered it in each other. Beyond life, beyond the grave and crematorium they were now risen above the Andes and the Alps, elevated above the words they no longer needed to squander. With their polemics and diatribes spent, they would no longer argue who was God's or the devil's agent, rather who, at night, as they sprawled leg over leg, would be the embraced and who the embracer; love would once again render them into merging contraries. One day, imagined Tintin, in some café or library, or in a common study, or in the amplitude of a shared wide bed, the sundering words would begin again, and the ancient schism would rupture them anew; or spent and aging, they would die together, in mutual compact, painlessly, by pill or gas, or the letting of veins, by means ensuring that one would not outlive the other, by means that would bind them, as they were now bound, arm in arm, through eternity. All that was still to come, but for the moment the generous days were just unfolding.

For himself now, Tintin thought, there was ahead only the memory of love and the path which it flowered.

# Chapter XXI

[That night.]

It was already dusk when Lieutenant dos Amantes came to fetch him from the hotel.

"We have some matters to discuss, Señor Tintin."

"Yes, I've been waiting."

"You know already?"

"Much of it. As I once recently learned you formed a part of my unfolding history, this morning I realized that you had something further to reveal to me."

"*Bueno.* So far it is as it should be."

"Are you frightened, my lieutenant?" Tintin asked gently.

"I have been for some time, ever since meeting the fat one who died, your precursor. I have had many doubts and apprehensions. I feel myself unworthy of this."

"You derive from a long line of those who have waited in solitude. Your worthiness is in your blood."

"I'm grateful to you, Señor Tintin. At times a man needs reassurance. It is so difficult to live."

"Yes."

The two departed as if on signal. Walking side by side, in

minutes they reached the ridge connecting the ruined city to Huayna Picchu, crossed, and slowly ascended the mountain ledge to the pinnacle. Three thousand feet below them the Urubamba River glimmered in the last light of the sun, and beyond, the green jungle gathered the humid darkness from the sky.

Lieutenant dos Amantes unfastened his cartridge box, drew out from it a jaguar-skin pouch, and spilled three dry mushrooms into his palm.

"Señor Tintin, these are for you to eat, slowly. They are the most potent of all the highland fungi known to the Inca high priests before the conquest. The secret of their existence was transmitted to only a few in each succeeding generation. We have been waiting for him, the special one, to savor them. It is for you—I think—we have waited. Now I have done my part. What you learn here tonight shall decide the rest."

"Yes, my good lieutenant, this is the way I, too, have come to understand it," said Tintin, nibbling on a mushroom stem.

"I shall leave after the mushroom starts cooking in you. No matter what you see or hear, do not be frightened or try to return to the hotel; the descent would be perilous. You will not know the hours passing, and you will not be cold or uncomfortable, and in any case, that is of little matter. I shall return to escort you in the morning."

"Don't worry, Lieutenant. It's you should take care, for there is a snake by your left elbow. A snake of two minds. He thinks he would like to sting you, for your presence offends him; he thinks, too, that you're not worth the effort."

"Is he a large serpent, Tintin?"

"No, very small and thin, and with two heads. A lemon-green wand in coil, his mouths the color of pomegranate, his fangs speckled blue and white, his eyes like flecks of black diamonds."

"Will I die, my friend?"

"Not tonight, he has decided. Do leave now. I would speak to this creature."

"Good night, my hope," the lieutenant said passionately, exhilarated by the fulfillment of this new stage of the prophetic design: the reappearance of this unusual serpent and Tintin's powers to fathom the creature's thoughts.

The moon illumined Lieutenant dos Amantes's stumbling but cautious way down along the narrow ledge, led him beaconlike ultimately back to his room, where alone in bed, he praised the miracle of man's solidarity with the earth, and he prayed for life's greater wisdom to visit him until finally his prayers spun him to deepest sleep.

Tintin considered his conversation with the snake dull. The serpent, Tintin discovered, knew little more of the world than the scope of the mountaintop on which he dwelled.

"I marvel, serpent, that for one so beautiful and rare there is so little to you at heart."

"Do you take form for substance?"

"Yes. Since recently. But I'm losing the notion as quickly as I acquired it. You are good argument for my revision. Be off, friend. I expect more telling visitors presently."

"Certainly, Tintin," said the snake, suddenly sprouting wings and golden plumes. Tintin followed his gliding flight into the absorbing darkness.

Suddenly Tintin was seated in a theater, third row, center aisle. The lights dimmed. A fat, grinning man in a crisp tuxedo bowed to the audience (Tintin was the only spectator) and, after pausing for a moment as if in acknowledgment of general applause, spoke: "Tonight, ladies and gentlemen, and for this night only—never to be performed again in the whole of the Americas—we are honored to present for your amusement and edification, and employing the greatest talents— man and beast—ever assembled on one stage, the Grand Spectacle of the New World. Without further delay, and with the request that you hold your applause until the show is completed, I ask that the curtain be raised and our evening begin.''

A shaky spotlight followed the impresario as he edged into the wings. "The Mexican Hat Dance" struck up on a phonograph, and presently two dancers emerged doing a heel-and-toe step. No sooner had they reached stage center (and the elegant mustachioed caballero tossed his sombrero to the floor) than the music stopped and the spotlight went dead. When the beam reappeared, some seconds later, it struck its vermilion glow on the impresario, dressed this time in the costume of a gaucho of the pampas, a bola suspended from his kerchiefed neck, a gleaming dirk stuck in the fold of a green silk sash about his large belly. Bowing and waving his hands as if to plead with the audience to halt its applause, he began introducing the next act, but a squad in cuirasses and helmets, rapiers drawn before their eyes, interrupted him. They marched briskly across the stage, followed by a short man straddling a stuffed brown horse pulled by wires attached to its dusty forelegs.

"Pizarro and his valiant band en route to Peru," announced the master of ceremonies, sidestepping the onslaught of horse and rider.

Dressed in cardboard armor, his false black beard strung perceptibly about his ears, Pizarro held in one hand the standard of Spain, which fell limply to the pole, and in the other, a long silver-painted wooden sword. The conquistador kept his head high and his eyes fixed nobly ahead, as if viewing the prospect of his future victories and glory in the theater wings to which he was being slowly dragged.

Lights down. Sounds of shuffling and of props being moved, thuds and noisy curses. Lights up.

The Inca, in full headdress and ceremonial robes lies prone, bound to a stone bed. Pizarro stands by as his men torture the man. One removes the Inca's headdress and ties a thin braided cord about his forehead; he inserts a stick under the cord and twists the tourniquet slowly. Others, with papier-mâché fires, roast the Inca's already charred feet. Gold tears stream from the Inca's ears and mouth.

Throughout the night many acts and *tableaux vivants* of similar historical nature followed. Tortures, murders, conversions of Indians at the stake, kidnappings, transportations and enslavements, whippings, mutilations, the murders and extinction of tribes by the Spanish invaders—bodies strewn into rivers and pits or left to beasts and birds.

The *tableaux vivants* vanished, and a huge screen dropped before the stage. Images rushed by at kaleidoscopic pace. Tintin saw vast settlements spring before his eyes where forests, ripped from their roots, had once swayed. Tractors cut swaths into the living green forest. Hills of trees young and old, brush and bush and all living creatures caught in the teeth of the invading machine burned, the flames alighting the surrounding forest and transforming it into a furious crackling furnace, fat smoke billowing into a black tent high in the sky. Highways unfurled like carpets of concrete over the tracks of raw burned earth, and new steel-and-concrete settlements rose beside great rivers and deep into the jungle where once only jaguars lived. The great rivers and lakes turned brackish and spewed dead grinning fish. Trees and undergrowth were uprooted and swept away in the rains that flooded the stripped land, and when the earth baked in the scorching sun, the rich soil turned to bitter sand where nothing grew. Many went hungry and died, some died eating the earth, little mustaches of powdery film ringing lips and chin.

When Lieutenant dos Amantes rejoined Tintin as the sun's first rays blazed over the mountaintops, the officer found the young man asleep, his hand over his mouth, just as he had left it, to stifle a yawn.

"Tintin, wake," the lieutenant implored.

"Why, yes! Most instructive, most, simply elucidating," the young man answered energetically to the officer's anxious call.

"Is that all? Instructive? Elucidating?"

"Of course, there are other things, too," Tintin added gravely, "added attractions, I mean. Let's say our farewells and be off, Lieutenant, I must have an early morning start."

"¿Nada más?" the lieutenant asked, his voice sunken low. "From all you have been privileged to see and learn, you leave me and my hopes with so little?"

The disappointment on the lieutenant's face pierced Tintin.

"Yes, there is more to say, which you and your goodness deserve, my lieutenant: Know that 'the earth revolves, men are born, live their time and die; communities are formed and are dissolved; dynasties appear and disappear; good contends with evil and evil still has its day; the whole, however, advancing slowly but unerringly toward the great consummation, which was designed from the beginning and which is certain to arrive in the end. . . . The supreme folly of the hour is to imagine that perfection will come before its stated time.' "

"Well, then, Señor Tintin," the lieutenant said, "let us now truly be on our way."

# Chapter XXII

[One month later. Lima. Dusk.]

On the Plaza de las Armas, near Lima's antique cathedral, where Don Francisco Pizarro's leathery corpse lies in an alcove, protected from the touch of the curious and the ravages of polluting air by an enclosed glass vault, on this plaza where Tintin sat cross-legged, begging his meal, passed at dusk a woman in a Castilian mantilla and jeweled peña, her long, close-fitting black dress swirling along the pavement.

"*¿Qué pasa?*" her sleek-haired, youthful companion inquired as she paused before the mendicant.

"*Nada, aspereme un momentito,*" she replied, leaving his side to address the bearded and tattered young man. "It is you, isn't it?"

"Someone like that," answered Tintin, slowly lifting his eyes to Clavdia Chauchat's troubled face.

"I think of you often, Tintin. And do you me?"

"When I feel ill, since you are my illness."

"As for myself," the woman hissed, "ever since the calamity, 'nothing is left me but to brood, brood, all day, all night in unprofitable longings and repinings.' I cannot be with you, or with myself. I'm emptied. Since you cannot kill my emptiness, kill me, its vessel."

"I would kill you if it would help you. It is an indifferent matter to me, killing you now. Once I would have killed us both; once, after the merge, I would have done it with all the passion of my humanized heart. I would have killed us with such love that all the uncombined elements of this world would have envied our union. To kill our flesh and join in spirit, how I longed for that once.

"But not today. Do not ask now, 'Tintin, kill me.' Say, 'Tintin, *execute* me.' And I shall, as if you were some animal in pain. Shall I send a smooth bullet through your temple or heart? Shall I cave in your brains with Lima's curbstone? Say now, Clavdia, what to do, for there is yet some kindness in me to treat you with charity. Presently it will require your own lonely hand to do you this service and this mercy."

Clavdia stiffened. "Your new heart has acquired a taint of the vindictive, a taint making you truly human—grown-up, that is."

"Yes," said Tintin after a long, meditative pause. "You are right. I deplore my unkind words and the bitterness of my heart. Forgive me, Clavdia. Some lives are marked for sadness, and I have become so marked, though perhaps I shall emerge from this phase as I did from my former carefreeness. But for now the sadness in me is magnetlike and attracts the general misery of the world, sad for everything that exists, seeing, as I do, the metamorphosis of all things in creation. My eyes have gone alchemist, transmuting the smooth faces of children into the lines of their old age, seeing in the most youthful of mountains, raw, giant juniors of the earth, their decline to hills, boulders, rocks, pebbles, the crumbling away to mere sand, dust, and motes.

"Since all changes, all saddens me. I see the years slide you down the chute of eternity, a decay winnowing you from living to dead cells and thence to powder and vanishment. What will recriminations and broodings serve us then? Perhaps one day in the kind reach of eternity my indifferent atoms will circuit yours. Let us hope and strive for no more."

"Your words serve only to infuriate my blood—to use an expression you yourself might employ in your newly extravagant diction," Clavdia answered. "And because of your cruel words I elect to live and to outlive you. Let's see then how our little story finishes," Clavdia said, beckoning her pomaded escort from his impatient vigil.

Tintin looked on as the two entered the cathedral. Then, counting the coins in his hand, he made his way deeper and deeper into the city's slums.

# Chapter XXIII

[One month later. One hour after dawn. Belém, Brazil.]

A laundry shop some three meters from a quay on the eastern bank of the Pará, formerly the scene of much commercial activity, when cargo ships ran the river, holds loaded with rubber and coffee beans, ships from Europe and North America, from Iceland and Mozambique.

Tintin entered. The old Chinaman behind the counter studied the youth for some long moments, then rose and bowed.

"What language shall we speak?" the laundryman asked in Portuguese.

"Whichever you prefer," Tintin answered in Portuguese. "I hope I have not kept you waiting long," Tintin added.

"Waiting. Yes, I have been at that some while, but that is finished now. And now that you've come, I am free to return to my country; there are one or two old friends I wish to see."

"The good Lieutenant?" Tintin asked.

The Chinaman smiled. "Oh! Yes, he is one."

"That we should meet, that you possess the last link of knowledge between me and my fate, I have recently divined,"

Tintin said. "Let us now open and conclude our matter. I board the mailboat within the hour."

"Let boat and plans go," the Chinaman said gently, making preparations for tea.

Tintin excused himself for his rudeness and bowed to the older man. "Unfortunately there is still left in me some of the former self, which contrition and thought may yet purge," he said, bowing again.

"My prince," the Chinaman began, himself returning the bow, his face radiant, "I am to tell you..."

The Chinaman spoke until afternoon, when Tintin curled himself up on a mound of laundry and went to sleep. When he woke, it was dark; his companion had already lit the night lamps and had prepared tea and rice. Now they both spoke, their discussion drifting through the night but returning always to Tintin and to the revelations waiting for him.

# Chapter XXIV

Some say they saw Tintin at the mouth of the Tocantins, on a red riverboat plying the muddy stream. Bearded and suntanned, a silk green kerchief, the color of the rain forest wall, circling his neck, chameleon he had become. In some light his skin was honey and copper; in other light, pale yellow; and in the shade of a tree or beside the wall of a river mud hut, purple-black.

Whatever his color, all welcomed him and were honored by his visit: The sick were cured by his healing touch; the blind had sight; the mute spoke; the tormented were calmed. Many spoke of his special fondness for dogs, the rheumy and the quick, and how they would greet him in the villages, barking an exultant howl, and rush among themselves for his gentle words and caress. But he was no stranger to all the breeds and races of plants and animals. The shy mimosa opened at his glance; the spiky maguey drooped at his touch, its barbs turned soft and pliant. Of all the creatures he encountered or that came deliberately to see him, the mole and the anaconda, the tapir and the spider monkey, the eagle and her nervous children, of them all, the jaguar he heeded most.

He spent hours in their lairs, preaching to them during their bloody, jaguar repasts the virtue of leaf and grass, for it was known he ate only that which grew in the soil and turned to the sun. He was, many in the villages said, the jaguars' prince.

He crossed the Gran Chaco on foot, paddled his way in a *batelão* up the Pilcomayo, following the trail of the explorers Crevaux and Ibaretta and Thouar, the Frenchman, who had made the perilous journey from the Upper Pilcomayo to Asunción on the Río Paraguay, and there on the salty swamps of the middle-river journey, he sojourned with the fierce Tobas, whom he taught the use of rare plants and herbs that cured the suffering and disease the chill south wind always blew them. On his departure the Indians trained women and children in the lost art of the blowgun and began to set large stores of poison to tip their arrows and shafts. Passing through the vast hardwood *quebracho* forests in the southern part of the Chaco, Tintin lived among the native workers in the tannin factories, addressing the men during siesta on the virtues of the noble, stately trees from which they drew their meager subsistence, explaining that presently the timber would be all gone, the way of the brazilwood, the distant redwood.

"Noble they are, noble, quite—your brothers." Some workers armed with rifles quit the factories and ranged the hardwood tracts, preaching to the loggers the virtues of the forests and threatening to shoot their overseers. Production halted temporarily.

On June 21, the Inca festival of the sun, two thousand tribes, many who had never known the existence of the others and others who had been ancient, murderous enemies, joined in harmonious union, gathering in a vast plain where many rivers crossed: the Xingús with their stone axes and knives made from the teeth of the piranha, the passive Muras of the lower Amazon, their bodies caked black with river mud to protect them against mosquitoes, the Yuracarés from the banks of the Río Chaparé in eastern Bolivia, with bow and long arrows, the seminomadic Zaparos from the Napo Valley in Ecuador, Salome Indians from the state of Morales, Mexico, in white suits and huaraches, bearing Winchesters and machetes, the plateau and mountain people of the Andean plateau and the Cordillera Real, the remnants of the ferocious Argentine pampa tribes exterminated by General Roca in 1879; sullen and silent, the remaining fifteen Tehuelches of the Patagonian plains, who practiced throwing the bola, the Caraios of the Orinoco basin, who carried blowguns and grenades in their long war canoes. Standing on a knoll at a crossing of several giant rivers, his arms outstretched in a gesture of embrace, Tintin addressed the multitude in a forgotten ancient language once common to all tribes, a language they suddenly, joyously recalled, and he shared with them his vision.

Some weeks later, alone once again, Tintin sat cross-legged by a grassy embankment, regarding the Amazon for three days. When, at last, he could see all the algae and the amoebas and spirogyras, when he could see all the microscopic cells and their molecules and the molecules of water and its atoms, the two of hydrogen and the one circuit of oxygen, when he could see the neutrons, protons, electrons, and the stars brilliantly shining beyond them like a vast wall of blue shimmering and pulsating through the universe, he undressed completely—except for a red macumba pouch strung about his neck—immersed himself in the water, and streamed away into the ribboned darkness and light.